SHAM

SHAM

ROGER SILVERWOOD

THORNDIKE
CHIVERS

This Large Print edition is published by Thorndike Press, Waterville, Maine, USA, and by BBC Audiobooks Ltd, Bath, England.

Thorndike Press is an imprint of The Gale Group

Thorndike is a trademark and used herein under license.

LIBRARY OF CONGRESS CATALOGING-IN-PUBLICATION DATA

Silverwood, Roger.
    Sham / by Roger Silverwood.
        p. cm. — (Thorndike Press large print clean reads)
    ISBN-13: 978-0-7862-9883-9 (alk. paper)
    ISBN-10: 0-7862-9883-9 (alk. paper)
        1. Police — England — Yorkshire — Fiction. 2. Yorkshire (England) —
Fiction. 3. Large type books. I. Title.
PR6069.I365S53 2007
823'.914—dc22   2007026775

BRITISH LIBRARY CATALOGUING-IN-PUBLICATION DATA AVAILABLE

Published in 2007 in the U.S. by arrangement with Robert Hale Limited.
Published in 2008 in the U.K. by arrangement with Robert Hale Limited.

U.K. Hardcover: 978 1 405 64248 4 (Chivers Large Print)
U.K. Softcover: 978 1 405 64249 1 (Camden Large Print)

Printed in the United States of America on permanent paper
10 9 8 7 6 5 4 3 2 1

SHAM

ONE

The Elms, Wallasey Road, Liverpool, Mersey-side, UK. Monday, 9 May

'Just lean back on ze pillow, Mrs Rossi. Relax. That's it. . . . Are you feeling drowsy?'

The busty ex-model with the long auburn hair nodded. She had cheekbones higher than the Hanging Gardens of Babylon, and a nose and nostrils the shape of the gold cast taken from the death mask of Cleopatra.

'I feel strange,' she said. 'I feel very strange.' She lifted her head up from the operating table, opened her eyes and glared at the bald little man in the thick glasses and white coat, hovering over her.

'Should I feel strange?' she demanded, suspiciously. 'I have never felt like this before.'

'Just relax. It'll be the sedative, that's all,' the doctor replied, putting his hand gently on her shoulder to ease her back down on the operating table.

She stiffened, breathed in noisily, pulled away from him, glared at his fat red fingers then stared at him with eyes like Medusa.

He took in her reaction. His mouth dropped open and he withdrew his hand instantly.

'Don't manhandle me, doctor,' she said icily.

His pasty white cheeks flushed the colour of the final notice he had had from the Inland Revenue that morning, and his stomach felt like he'd swallowed a couple of frogs hell bent on filling a jam jar with spawn. The touch was entirely innocent. He felt foolish and breathed out a long silent sigh.

The skirmish served to remind him that he was dealing with a very, *very* dangerous woman.

She settled back on the pillow. Her eyes closed.

There were a few seconds of uncomfortable silence.

Doctor Schumaker pursed his lips. He needed to lighten the atmosphere; the patient shouldn't be tense. He managed a smile.

'Yes. Yes. That's all right,' he said eventually. 'Relax. You need to be as relaxed as possible. There, there. Now it won't hurt. You'll hardly feel anything. Just lean back against the pillow, that's it, yes. Think of something nice; think of how much more beautiful you are going to look, when we are finished. You'll have men falling at your feet.'

'They already fall at my feet,' she growled.

His left eyebrow lifted then dropped.

'Yes. Yes. You'll look as beautiful as ze statue, de Venus de Milo!'

'I know. And I do.'

His jaw tightened. He licked his lips.

'Tink how much you are going to give those young girls a run for their money.'

'Don't be ridiculous,' she snarled. 'I have five homes in the UK and one in the States. I have two limos. I have a husband and two sons and a granddaughter. I am not a young tart who hangs around hotel bars and shoves cards in telephone boxes, to earn fifty quid a drop!'

Schumaker blinked.

'No. No. No, of course not,' he said quickly and then licked his lips. 'You know I didn't mean that, Mrs Rossi.'

'I know I only look half my sixty years,' she said and it was true. 'But I just want to make the best of myself. *So get on with it.*'

The doctor pursed his lips. He must be

careful not to show what he really thought.

'I just mean that you are going to be as beautiful as the most beautiful of them.'

She closed her eyes and wrinkled up her nose as though she could smell twelve jurymen about to cry, 'guilty'.

'Yeah. Yeah.'

There was a rattle of metal against glass as the doctor rolled open a canvas holdall. He found a small bottle and stuck a hypodermic into it; he held it up to the light and pulled down the plunger. He glanced down at her as the pale yellow liquid began to fill the syringe.

Her eyes were still closed and she seemed relaxed.

He sighed.

'That's it, Mrs Rossi,' he said in a practised monotone. 'That's it. Go to sleep. Think beautiful. Think beautiful torts. Think warm beaches, blue green seas, gentle svishing of ze tide coming in and then falling back. That's it, that's it.'

Her eyelids suddenly clicked open.

'I can't sleep,' she snapped. 'It's no good. I can't sleep.'

She saw him move over her with a hypodermic in his hand.

'Have those instruments been sterilized?' she snapped. 'I won't have dirty needles

10

used on me.'

'It's a brand new needle, Mrs Rossi. Brand new. Straight out of sterile wrapping. Don't vorry. I don't take any chances. Now please, lean back . . . close your eyes and relax. Have confidence. Trust me. There is nothing to vorry about.'

She glanced at him, turned the corners of her mouth down while wrinkling the nose upwards, and flopped back on to the pillow.

His fingers trembled slightly as he tucked the white sheet neatly back under her chin.

He was about to beautify a valuable, cash paying client: wife of one of Britain's most notorious murderers, bank robbers and fix-ers.

He hadn't wanted the job. He hadn't needed the work. Rikki Rossi had rolled up outside his house with a couple of heavies and demanded his services. Schumaker only agreed because he was too scared to refuse. The Rossis had a terrifying reputation and the doctor had taken a liking to living. He had got used to it. The money was all right. Twenty thousand pounds in cash. For a total of around eight hours work spread over ten weeks. Payment on completion. A piece of cake. He had already planned to winter in the Maldives again and he was looking forward to it.

However, he found that there was no pleasure in the work. He would have been far happier, nipping, tucking, enlarging and reducing the host of would be starlets and has-been celebrities that had kept his appointment book more or less full the last twenty years.

'Well, what are you waiting for?' she suddenly bawled.

'For the sedative to work. You must keep very still. Very still, Mrs Rossi. And keep calm.'

'I am calm!' she snapped.

His left eye twitched. He swallowed and pulled the powerful light down closer to her face. He picked up a pair of powerful magnifying spectacles, settled them on his nose and threaded the sides round his ears.

'Hmmm. These are the same hands that helped Gloria Van Struman come first in the European Beauty Championship of 2003,' he said, as he pulled on the rubber gloves. 'And I was the von who made the granddaughter of an Ethiopian goat farmer so irresistible to Lord Henry Pennington-Bookbinder that he proposed to her on their very first meeting. She is now Lady Pennington-Bookbinder, heiress of the Blue Crescent shipping line and half the Caribbean. Modesty prevents me from citing the many others I have had the pleasure of including among my patients . . . royalty, film stars, beauty queens, models . . . from all over ze world. I could go on.'

'Yes,' she said with a sneer. 'You *do* go on,' she added wryly.

His mouth went dry.

He coughed and said: 'Now please keep still.'

'I am still! Get on with it!' she fumed.

He swallowed.

'When I have finished, Mrs Rossi,' he said, as his trembling hand reached out to the corner of her mouth, 'I promise you, you will take your husband's breath away!'

She opened one eye and glared at him.

'And if you stick that needle in the wrong spot, Schumaker,' she replied sourly. 'I promise you: *he* will take *your* breath away . . . permanently!'

A cold shiver ran down the doctor's back.

King William Street, Streatham, London, UK.
Friday, 29 July
The Northern National Bank opened its doors as usual promptly at 9.30 a.m. and three young women and a man who were standing on the front steps turned and moved inside.

At 9.32 am, three grey-haired men arrived at the bank from different directions. They went through the door and slowly made their way to the tellers' windows. They were followed in by a woman stooping and wearing a headscarf that also covered her mouth. She carried a bulging plastic Tesco shopping-bag that appeared to be heavy. She struggled with it through the double doors on to the tiled area just inside the bank, where, suddenly, it appeared to split open. Coins tumbled out, making a loud noise and rolling in every direction around the bank floor. Everybody turned to see what was happening. The woman stared at the pile of coins in dismay then bent forward to begin to collect them up. Nobody, including the grey-haired men, seemed inclined to leave their places in the queue at the tellers' windows to assist her.

A young woman clerk from behind the tellers' partition heard the noise and peered through the glass. She went to the door to the foyer and peered carefully through the security spy-hole. Seeing nobody close by, she opened it carefully and rushed out to help the woman.

One of the three grey-haired men, standing only ten feet away, threw a handful of bean bags he had concealed in his pockets at the open doorway. Some landed between the door and the jamb preventing the door from closing and locking. He rushed to it, pushed it wide open and was in the tellers' area and next to the tills in a second. Another of the grey-haired men followed right behind him.

The first man pulled out a Walther PPK/S automatic from his waistband and waved it in the air. 'Everybody stand still. Don't move. Hands in the air, where I can see them,' he bawled savagely.

The third man pulled out a revolver and stood in the foyer by the street door. Meanwhile, the woman near the entrance, who had dropped the money, leapt to her feet, abandoned the scattered coins and dashed out of the bank at surprising speed.

The young woman clerk, realizing what she had allowed to happen, put a hand to her mouth, let out a small gasp and stood shaking, looking anxiously at the armed man.

The second man took out a black plastic bin-liner from his pocket and opened it up.

'Fill that sack,' the gunman yelled. 'Just the paper. No coins. Hurry up.'

Nobody moved.

The tellers, clerks and customers stood frozen to the spot and stared at the three men. They could now see that they were wearing skin-tight masks and grey wigs and, by their movements, observed that they were much younger than they had at first appeared.

'Move it!' the first gunman yelled and angrily fired a shot at the wall. A shower of dust fell across the counter into a woman teller's hair. Her jaw dropped open, her big eyes grew bigger.

Bells suddenly began to ring, both inside and outside the bank. The racket made the walls and floor vibrate.

The gunman spun round through 180 degrees and back, waving the Walther in the air.

A man at the back made a swift move.

The gunman saw him and fired a shot.

The clerk's face showed pain, his eyes closed, he collapsed, arms in the air, hitting his face on a desk as he fell. A small trickle of blood ran from the side of his head.

A girl screamed, some others gasped.

'*Fill that sack,*' the gunman shrieked again and fired another shot at the ceiling.

A woman teller promptly leaned over her till and began rapidly pulling out the paper money and dropping it into the black sack.

The others hurriedly followed her lead and began to unload their till drawers and reserve stock underneath, thrusting bundles of wrapped notes of all denominations at the man.

'Hurry up! Hurry up!' the gunman bawled and fired another shot, above the head of a teller who was not moving fast enough for him.

Twenty seconds later, the money stopped flowing. The tills were empty. The bank staff straightened up, put their hands above their heads and stood motionless, their hands shaking in the air.

The second man closed up the neck of the sack, and dashed out into the foyer. The gunman followed. They joined the third man.

The three of them rushed into the street together. The bells seemed even louder outside. The two men with guns waved them in the air.

A small throng of eighteen or twenty sightseers had gathered on the pavement at the opposite side of the road; there were a few exclamations as the men appeared. They edged back rapidly at the sight of the guns.

A high-powered black car promptly raced up to the bank doors. The brakes squealed. It was being driven by the woman who had minutes earlier noisily managed the discharge of the bag of coins in the bank entrance. The grey wig and headscarf were still in place.

The three men jumped into the car. The engine roared. The car disappeared round the corner of the building as the doors were being slammed shut.

Two men dashed out of the bank door and looked round.

Seconds later, a police car arrived on the scene at speed, its siren blaring, blue lights flashing. The co-driver spoke briefly to one of the men and the car sped off in the direction of the black car.

Another police car arrived, sirens blaring, and a third, then an ambulance arrived.

Five minutes later, the body of a man covered by a bloody sheet was brought out of the bank on a stretcher.

Coronation Park, Bromersley, South Yorkshire, UK. 8.30 p.m. Sunday, 31 July
Mirabelle looked wistfully into his eyes as they sauntered holding hands in the warm summer evening.

'But I hardly know you,' she whispered, and then opened and closed her moist lips several times intriguingly.

The young man smiled.

'What is there to know? You know that I

love you.'

She returned the smile, then shook her head.

They drifted through the park in silence, taking in the dimming blue sky, the trees in full leaf and the long stretches of carefully maintained grassy areas around them. They passed between some thick bushes that developed into an avenue of cypresses.

'It was a lovely meal,' she said at length. She put a hand to her temple. 'But I think the wine has gone to my head,' she added, with a smile.

'My flat is only a few yards from the park gates, Mirabelle. We can be there in a few minutes,' he said gently. 'You could rest there awhile.'

She gave him an old-fashioned look.

He smiled back. Then he spotted a bench in an alcove of squarely cut privet. He raised his eyebrows and pointed to it. She nodded and they sat down. She snuggled up close to him. She shivered slightly. The pristine sleeveless summer dress did not afford much warmth. He took off his jacket and draped it round her shoulders.

She looked up into his clear brown eyes.

'Thank you,' she murmured sweetly.

'Now I've got you, I have to look after you.'

'Who would think, I have only known you a week,' she said.

'What does time matter, Mirabelle,' he said. He took her hand and squeezed it slightly.

She sighed.

He sighed.

There was a quiet moment.

Suddenly an empty lager can came flying through the air and landed on the pathway in front of them; it bounced and rolled towards their feet.

They sat upright, astonished, and looked round.

A young man in a black T-shirt and tight jeans leaped on to the path from behind a bush with a dangerous-looking knife in his hand. He stood leaning forward, with his feet spread apart in the stance of a challenger.

'What does time matter,' he said mockingly, attempting to imitate the voice of the young man. 'What does time matter,' he repeated. 'Well, your time has come, mate. That girl is mine.'

Mirabelle stared at him and gasped. She noticed the careful and detailed representation of a skull and crossbones in blue on the back of his hand.

'I don't know you,' she cried. 'Leave us alone!'

The young man stood up, faced him and assumed a similar stance. He eyed the long glinting knife studiously. It looked like a kitchen knife with a pointed tip. He had nothing to defend himself against it.

The intruder stared at the young man, smiling, but his eyes showed only his enthusiasm for a fight.

'What do you want with me?' the young man said boldly.

The intruder advanced, stabbing strongly and dangerously into the air.

'That girl's mine,' he snarled.

The young man dodged his attacks deftly by backing off and moving in a circular direction, arriving with his back to the park bench.

Mirabelle screamed. Her lips quivered. Her eyes glowed brightly with fear. She leapt up from the bench and moved behind it for safety. The suit coat he had so gallantly put round her shoulders slid on to the bench.

The intruder advanced more strongly.

'I'll have you, you swine!'

The young man made another quick step back with his right foot. Out of his eye corner, he noticed his coat on the seat. He reached out for it and lashed it wildly around the intruder's head.

The intruder grinned and reached out to try to grab hold of it, but didn't get a hold.

The young man then threw it in his face.

Momentarily, the intruder's view was obstructed; he lunged blindly with the knife into the air.

This time the young man managed to grab his wrist with both hands and he squeezed it and squeezed it.

With his free hand, the intruder hurled a mighty succession of blows to the young man's head. He reeled but hung on tightly to the wrist. As they struggled, both men lost their balance and landed on the hard concrete path.

Mirabelle screamed again.

The young man squeezed the intruder's wrist with a grip of steel and banged his hand repeatedly on the concrete. Four, five, six times.

'Drop it! Drop it!' he demanded.

The intruder continued landing blows to the young man's head, but he hung on regardless and banged the intruder's wrist on the concrete again and again.

The intruder's fingers suddenly opened. The gleaming blade with the black handle dropped on to the path.

The young man reached out, snatched it up, put his knee on the intruder's chest and held the weapon at his throat momentarily.

Mirabelle screamed.

It seemed he thought better of it. He held it behind his back and got to his feet.

'Get up,' he said, panting and pulling the intruder up by his shirt.

Mirabelle sighed. She put her hands to her face.

The two men stood facing each other, red faced and struggling for breath.

The young man released his grip on the man's shirt and wiped his mouth with the back of his hand. The intruder looked quickly at his bruised hand, then without a word, dashed off behind the bushes and was soon out of sight.

The young man made to follow him, when Mirabelle rushed forward from behind the bench, her arms outstretched to embrace him.

'No. Let him go. Are you all right, my darling?'

'Yes. Yes, oh yes.'

'You were wonderful.'

He put his hands on her waist and shrugged.

She kissed him passionately on the lips, and even as they separated they came back together several times, then hugged each other, snuggling closer and closer.

'Did you say your flat was close by?' she said, her chest heaving.

He smiled and pulled her back to him again.

Two

Wakefield Prison, North Yorkshire. 3.15 p.m. Friday, 30 December

'You're very late, Mrs Buller-Price,' Prison Officer Elloughton said, gently chiding her, as he closed the heavy door and turned the key. 'I thought you weren't coming. I'm afraid you won't be allowed any extra time. Rules is rules, you know.'

She pursed her lips tightly and shook her head briefly.

'Tut tut, Mr Elloughton, I know all that. This is my third year as a prison visitor,' she puffed and settled her big frame into the little wooden chair facing the empty table. 'I'm quite familiar with the rules and regulations, even though there *are* so many of them. No. No. It was my car, you see. It has let me down. I hope I haven't upset Mr Rossi.'

'Do him good, if you have,' he said callously.

'Oh no, Mr Elloughton,' she said disapprovingly, shaking all four chins. 'You shouldn't say that. I am only allowed once a month and only for two hours, so time is very precious to him.'

Elloughton frowned thoughtfully then shook his head.

'Well, I've sent for him already,' he said. 'He should be here directly.'

'Ah, good. Thank you. I've brought him some scones and a sponge cake. They are in there,' she said pushing a large white paper bag towards him. 'If you would be so kind. And a bar of fruit and nut. And forty cigarettes. Although I fail to understand why the government is happy to encourage prisoners to die of lung cancer by permitting them cigarettes, but totally forbids them to die of alcohol poisoning.'

He picked up the bag, nodded and smiled. 'I'll put them in the book and see he gets them.'

'Thank you so very much, Mr Elloughton,' she said with a cherubic smile.

There was the sound of footsteps and a rattle of keys and the heavy room door opened.

'That'll be him now. He'll have to go back at straight up four, though, you know. Sorry.'

He went out through the door behind her

and she heard the door lock.

'Yes. Yes,' she muttered to herself. 'Rules is rules,' she added and wrinkled her nose.

She looked ahead across the table at the far door expectantly, and deliberately assumed a smile to greet the man. It was opened by a prison officer who followed the door round with the key still in the lock.

A big man stood framed in the doorway. He almost filled it. He looked across at Mrs Buller-Price, nodded and stepped forward. He was about sixty years of age and dressed in denims. He had a head like a sack of potatoes, dropped on a neck as thick as a telegraph pole. He rolled slowly up to the table, then slumped in the chair, glanced at her, yawned and put his hands in his pockets.

The prison officer pulled the door to and locked it. They were alone.

She began with a huge smile.

'Ah. Dear Mr Rossi, I am most dreadfully sorry to be late. I know that our little chats every month are so valuable to you and enable you to while away the lonely hours more easily after I have gone. I am most dreadfully sorry to say that our time, alas, will be limited today because my dear car, my beloved Bentley has let me down. It is, of course, getting on a bit . . . like me . . .

dear me . . . yes. It was bought by my husband in 1976, just before he died, and has served us very well. I vowed I would keep it and run it as long as I could, but I fear it may be in need of a major repair. But what actually happened was that I had finished taking the milk down to the lane end on the little trolley and had hoisted the churns on to the collection platform as usual, fed the dogs, changed my shoes and coat, got the baking off the slab, put it in the back of the car and went to start it and, blow me, I couldn't get a peep out of it. I tried and tried. Eventually, I phoned my friend Mr Lestrange at the garage, he came out promptly with a battery, coupled it up and did things, but it still wouldn't start. Meanwhile, of course, the clock was ticking and I was thinking of you. Anyway, he towed it down to his workshop, with me steering. It was jolly hard, I can tell you. It's power steering and it was quite a struggle to take the corners. Anyway, he had a good look with his . . . whatever it is . . . and said it needed a new something or other; he'd have to get one, if he could. Being such an old model, he wasn't sure. Meanwhile I would be without transport. That was quite a blow. Well, dear Mr Rossi, I live out in the country you may know. To be without a car out there is a minor disaster. I'll have to take a taxi everywhere. And they are not always available to me. One would have to come all the way out from Bromersley, that's five miles away and the meter would have started out there too. Anyway, I said I would need a taxi to bring me here immediately. He rang round from his garage but there was no one available instantly to come out to Tunistone so Mr Lestrange himself agreed to bring me. And here I am, better late than never . . . with humble apologies, my dear Mr Rossi.'

Stefan Rossi nodded, looked at his watch and yawned again.

She smiled and said, 'Now then, Mr Rossi, you must tell me what sort of a month you've had. I thought of you, at my prayers at midnight mass and then afterwards, during Christmas day.'

He didn't reply.

'Well, I got back from church about one thirty in the morning. I don't pretend I was not a little nervous. Anyway, I have the dogs. I went to bed then. Very late for me, so I got up a little later. I must say it was very cold. I milked the cows and walked the dogs. Then I filled up the coal buckets. I didn't want to have to turn out again. I had a piece of steak which I cooked with a few onions and some carrots which was very nice. At a few minutes to three, I sat down; I listened to the queen's speech and opened a bottle of Chardonnay, those new wines are quite good, you know, no age, no body, but it was very good. I'm afraid I had a drop too much, and fell asleep in the chair. It was pitch black when I woke up. The television was blaring out some dreadful music. The fire was very low. I let the dogs out. There was a sinkful of pots I had to wash up and the pans. I went to bed. It was all jolly nice, though . . . if not a bit on the quiet side.'

Stefan Rossi didn't reply. He squinted at her through small, black piggy eyes from the lumpy face.

'Now, you must tell me what you did,' she continued. 'I hear you have decorations, and carols and a proper turkey dinner and everything.'

He nodded.

There was a pause.

'Good. Good. Hmmm. Now, Mr Rossi, it might be a bit difficult next month. If I don't get my car repaired and returned to me, if Mr Lestrange can't get the parts, I'm not quite sure how I will get here. It is all very worrying. But I will definitely come. Don't be worried about that. I will *definitely* be here. I will hire a car, if need be. So you are not to worry about that.'

Rossi yawned.

'Now, before I forget, are there any messages you want me to take out for you? To your wife or your family or friends or anybody? It's as well to keep in touch, you know. Anything you tell me will be in absolute confidence . . . you don't have to worry about that, you know.'

Stefan Rossi shook his head, hardly at all.

It was ten minutes past five on Monday morning, 2 January. The sky was as black as an undertaker's hat, as Mrs Buller-Price descended the farmhouse stairs carrying the beaker that had contained the previous night's drinking chocolate.

Her five dogs began to jump around and bark as they heard movement on the tread. They could always hear her progress however quietly she moved. She reached the stairs door, opened it and smiled as they crowded round her, barking and jumping up. She switched on the sitting-room light and they followed her, grateful for a simple acknowledgement of them in her soothing, comforting voice. She opened the door to the hall, made for the front door, turned the key and let them pour out into the yard. As she closed it and turned back, she felt something hard and unusual through her carpet slippers. She looked down. On the doormat there appeared to be a small key-ring with a key and something the size of a small matchbox, black and plastic, threaded on to it. She bent down, picked it up, and turned it over in her hand. She didn't recognize it. She pursed her lips. It didn't belong to her. It wasn't a key for the farm or any of her outbuildings or anywhere else she could think of. She looked back down at the carpet and then at the door. It had obviously been pushed through the letter-box. It must have been done quietly, very quietly, so quietly that the dogs had not been disturbed. She looked at the hall clock. It was just after 5.15 a.m. It had been dropped through the letterbox between ten o'clock or so the previous night and 5.15 a.m., the present time. She fingered the key-ring as she made her way towards the kitchen. She put the find on the kitchen worktop and switched on the electric kettle and the radio and thought no more about it.

She had breakfast, fed the dogs, scrubbed up for milking, donned her plastic apron, her big old coat, Wellington boots and waterproof hat, and made her way through the cool early morning darkness out of the farmhouse across the yard to the stable to milk and feed her six Jerseys.

An hour later, she was crossing the yard complete with the dogs, returning to the farmhouse for a recuperative cup of tea and a sit down, when she heard the powerful extension telephone bell, secured high up on the apex of the barn, ring out its loud, persistent jangle. She glanced up at it and wondered who could be calling at that unseemly hour; it must be an emergency of some sort. She increased her speed across the yard and into the house, becoming increasingly worried with each step she took. She observed from the hall clock that it was 7.25 as she passed it and made a beeline for the sitting-room, where she snatched up the phone.

'Yes. Alicia Buller-Price speaking. Who is this?' she said with a sense of foreboding.

A man's voice spoke very quickly and said, 'Ah yes. There's a car in your barn, love. Came up in the night. Didn't want to disturb you. We put the keys through your letterbox. It's there for you to test drive for a month or two . . . to see what you think. No obligation. Goodbye.'

There was a click and he'd gone. No opportunity for her to ask any questions.

She stood there, still holding the handset,

her mouth wide open, her head shaking. 'But I can't afford a new car,' she said indignantly, to nobody at all. She banged down the handset.

'Oh dear,' she said. The corners of her mouth turned downwards. 'Oh dear. Oh dear. Oh dear,' she said as she wandered into the kitchen. She saw the keyring with its appendages and snatched it up. She turned smartly and marched straight out of the house to the open barn where only three days ago her beloved Bentley had stood. Dawn was breaking, and in the early morning light she gasped as she saw a large, sleek, black limousine with shiny bonnet and doors, with a gleaming chromium-plated radiator grille and bumper.

Police Station, Bromersley, South Yorkshire. 8.28 a.m. Monday, 2 January

The solid steps of Detective Inspector Michael Angel echoed up the station corridor.

Cadet Ahmed Ahaz had been in the CID room listening out for his boss and he rushed to the door to waylay him.

'He's here, sir,' Ahmed said, urgently. 'I've seen him. He wants you to go to his office as soon as you come in.'

Angel stopped in the corridor, turned

34

slowly to face him, screwed up his eyebrows and began to unbutton his raincoat. 'Who? Who wants to see me?'

Ahmed's mouth dropped open.

'The new super, sir, DS Strawbridge. You hadn't forgotten. He starts here this morning . . . well, he's already started!' he said, his eyes popping out like a cartoon cat. 'He's in the old super's office.'

Angel wrinkled his nose and sniffed.

Ahmed was surprised that the inspector was so relaxed about the arrival of the new boss.

If truth be known, Angel wasn't as relaxed as he appeared. His predecessor, DS Harker, had been such a hard taskmaster, utterly charmless, mean and miserable, that he was delighted when he heard he had been promoted to Chief Constable in the Potteries somewhere and was glad to see the back of him. Of course, he was curious to see what sort of a man had been appointed his successor. He had heard that Strawbridge had come from the Smoke with something of a reputation as a crime fighter. He'd been made up one from a chief inspector. The change could only be an improvement, but he would have to see.

Angel nodded at Ahmed, removed his raincoat and threw it at him.

'Right,' he said turning towards the corridor.

He looked back.

'Finish that stuff on my desk and get it off to the Crown Prosecution Service. And rustle up some tea, smartish?'

'Right, sir,' Ahmed said, and bustled into the inspector's office with the coat.

Angel strode purposefully down the green corridor towards the superintendent's office. He sniffed and then sighed as he wondered what sort of chap this Strawbridge was going to turn out to be. He had worked under a dozen or more superintendents in his time but had never met one that he really liked. Of course, the force had changed a lot. It wasn't like it used to be. There were days he could recall when there was some fun in the place. Now it's full of rules and regulations, do's and don'ts, disagreeable customers as well as overbearing superiors. His father used to talk about camaraderie? There didn't seem to be much of that these days. He wrinkled his nose. Undertakers and rat catchers have more fun; he wondered what the going rate for a tail would be. He really didn't want to have to get to know a new face. Not that morning. He felt caught between a trip to the Inland Revenue and the dentist's. He arrived at the door, took in a deep breath and knocked on the door.

'Come in,' a determined voice called out.

He pushed open the door.

A big, tall, dark-suited man with a white, pock-marked face, and a thick head of dishevelled black hair, looked up from the desk at him. His eyes were black, small and cold.

'Come in,' he said, staring hard into Angel's eyes. He put down the file he had been reading, half stood up and held out his hand. 'You must be Michael Angel. I'm Strawbridge. Sit down. Sit down.'

Angel eyed the man carefully. His noticed that his mouth twisted into a leer when he tried to smile.

'Yes. Good morning, sir.'

He shook the hot, sticky hand and took the chair facing him. The desk was heaped with files and papers. Strawbridge sat down, nodded towards the file he had been reading. 'This is your file,' he said.

Angel nodded.

'You've had a lot of experience, I see,' he went on. 'And your father was in the force before you. Hmmm.'

Angel nodded again. What was there to say?

Strawbridge closed the file and dropped it

on to the desk. He looked into Angel's eyes a few seconds and then said, 'Well, inspector, I've got a very special job for you.'

Angel always liked to do something special, picked out for something . . . different. Sounded good. He wrinkled up his nose. Huh! Probably just a load of old cock robin.

'What's that, sir.'

Strawbridge tried for a smile again; it was difficult for him. He pursed his lips, then began: 'You'll have heard of the Rossis?'

Angel nodded.

It was already beginning to sound grim. That family was always bad news. The Rossis were one of the UK's elusive family of murderers, thieves and fixers, slippery as quicksilver, they came and they went. And nobody knew where they lived. They were reputed to have numerous homes and houses and properties, and daily flitted from one address to another, never sleeping in the same place two nights in succession. They had to dodge other gangs as well as the police. There were always jealousies and old scores to settle.

There was one Rossi behind bars, however. He was the eldest, Stefan Rossi. The family never visited him. But nevertheless, close contact was maintained. It was suggested that he ran the mob from behind the bars. He was never visited by any of them, for fear of being followed by a relay of police, eager beaver crime reporters or other mobsters. Addresses and rendezvous were always closely guarded secrets. Messages were passed by word of mouth, expensively paid for in cash or favours, or via mobile phones, frequently illegal in prison. No one ever knew how or who was carrying a message to or from one Rossi to another, in or out of prison. And no one dared to ask.

'Yes, sir. Stefan and Gina, father and mother, and Rikki and Carl, their sons. Manchester mob. Stefan's doing fourteen in Wakefield. Know of 'em. Not worked this part of Yorkshire, as far as we know anyway. Rikki shot a policeman, an inspector, in Castlecombe, further up Thirsk way. Rikki was caught and arrested, but couldn't make it stick. Had to let him go.'

'Yes. It's always been like that. But not this time. He's on remand in Manchester. Well I've got the young in-law . . . well, they were never married. But he was bunking up with Rikki Rossi's daughter, Sharon Rossi, his pride and joy. She was going steady with Pete Grady, more than two years. I got him, Pete Grady, willing to give evidence against Rikki . . . for murder.'

Angel's eyebrows shot up. Sounded good,

in fact, very good; quite a *coup.*

'What's the deal, sir?'

'No deal. You could say vengeance. It was Rikki that made Sharon give Grady the push. Grady didn't like it. Still doesn't.'

'You remember that cheeky robbery last October at the Northern City Bank in Streatham,' Strawbridge went on. 'Murdered a man. Bank clerk. Nasty. Got away with a hundred and ten thousand. Never found the cash.'

'Yes sir.'

'The Rossis pulled that job. Yes. Gina, their mother, was the queen bee, and the driver. Rikki and Carl and Pete Grady were the workers. But Grady says he wasn't armed. Says he didn't carry a gun. Furthermore, he says it was Rikki who pulled the trigger on that bank clerk. In fact, he's prepared to swear he did.'

Angel blinked and gave a little nod. This was indeed great stuff.

'Well it's time Rikki Rossi was put away. There are at least seven murders down to him. He's been working his way through the other criminals on his patch. Well, Rikki's on remand in Strangeways, well, it's just called plain Manchester these days. But I can't send him down without Pete Grady's evidence. Trial's in Manchester, case opens

Monday.'

'What do you want me to do, sir.'

'I want you to keep him hidden and alive until after the trial.'

'You mean in the safe house.'

Strawbridge shook his head.

'Police safe houses aren't safe enough.'

'Come in,' Angel bawled.

Ahmed came into the office gripping a tin tray with a beaker of tea wobbling precariously in the middle of it. He closed the door and turned to Angel who was busy at his desk.

'Ah. Ta,' Angel said, looking up. He quickly yanked open his desk drawer, pulled out a BT Broadband disc and slapped it down next to the telephone.

Ahmed carefully placed the beaker on it.

Angel picked it up, took a trial sip and winced.

'What is it? Turpentine?'

The cadet smiled wryly and shook his head. He knew the tea was good.

'Ahmed, I want you to get me the housing manager at the Town Hall. I reckon he owes me a favour, the amount I'm paying in community tax or whatever it's called these days.'

'The housing manager, sir? Is that his title?'

'Dunno. I want the chap who allocates council-owned rented flats or maisonettes in the borough.'

'Right, sir,' Ahmed said and turned to go. He wondered what the inspector wanted with a rented flat.

Suddenly, out in the corridor there was a loud scream. Sounded like a woman or a girl. It was a very loud scream. Then another.

They stared at the door.

The back of Ahmed's hand turned to goose-flesh.

'Sir!' he said and looked anxiously at the inspector.

Angel's fists tightened. He licked his lips.

'Better take a look.'

He jumped up, knocking the swivel chair back with the back of his legs.

The screaming continued; it was ear-piercing.

'Hurry up.'

Ahmed opened the door.

Angel charged out into the corridor.

The cadet followed close behind.

There was no immediate sign of anything or anybody. Four or five office doors opened in quick succession. Anxious faces looked out. Then, from the female locker room a WPC backed out into the corridor. It was clear to see that it was WPC Leisha Baverstock, the station beauty, in uniform but without a hat. She didn't look that beautiful at the moment. She was holding her face with both hands, and, as she turned, Angel could see her big eyes were bigger than ever; her mouth was open and her lips were quivering. She spotted Angel, turned rapidly towards him and wrapped her arms round his shoulders and crashed her head on to his chest.

Angel didn't move. He stood there motionless like Nelson on his column. It was unexpected.

'What is it, constable,' he eventually said, lamely. 'Erm . . . what's the matter, Leisha?'

She looked up into his face, blinked, pulled away from him and fished around in her pocket for something.

'Oh. Sorry, sir.' Then she pointed at the locker room door. 'It's in there,' she wailed. 'Under the sink.' She found a tissue and blew her nose.

'What is?'

'A rat, sir.'

'A rat! Is it dead?'

She squirmed.

'Oooo, no. No. Running up and down,'

she squealed.

Angel sniffed.

'How big is it?'

'Huge!' She held her finger and thumb two inches apart. 'With its tail, I reckon it'll be four inches long.'

Angel pulled a face.

'It'll be a field mouse. That won't hurt you.'

The nosey parkers down the corridor hanging out of the offices smiled, withdrew and closed their doors.

'I can't go back in there again, sir,' she said.

Two more WPCs appeared from up the corridor and gathered round the woman and began chattering animatedly.

Angel took the opportunity to escape. He turned and made his way down the corridor to his office.

'All that for a field mouse,' he muttered.

Ahmed caught up with him.

'Shouldn't we get a cat, sir?'

Angel blinked then shook his head.

'Would you condemn a cat to living in this mad house?'

As they walked back to the office, Ahmed considered the merits and demerits of being a cat living in Bromersley nick, while Angel recalled that he had heard screams like that

once in a bank siege, where a cornered gunman had shot an assistant bank manager.
He remembered the crack of the bullet and
the distressing reactions of the wife on being told. His mind then drifted into thinking about Pete Grady. . . .

THREE

The noon train from King's Cross pulled into Doncaster station at 13.32.

Michael Angel was standing on Platform 1, half concealed from the track by a telephone kiosk. He was pretending to read a copy of the *Financial Times,* inside which was tacked a four-year-old mugshot of Pete Grady.

The diesel rattled noisily up to the platform. People on the platform going to Leeds surged forward. Doors flew open as the train slowed and the passengers inside crowded at the top of the steps waiting for it to stop. He peered over the top of the paper and saw a familiar face on the top step of a carriage as it glided slowly past. It was not a face he had been expecting to see that afternoon. For a moment, he couldn't quite place it. He remembered it had been a long time since he had felt the owner's collar. The name came to him. Stuart Mace, gambling club proprietor, con man, bully-boy, extortionist and versatile villain extraordinaire, looking very prosperous: well-trimmed beard, sharp suit, umbrella, expensive suitcase. What was he doing back here? He had thought he had left South Yorkshire for sunnier climes. Well, it was a free country: it was a public railway station, and he had served his time. He watched the bearded Stuart Mace step off the moving train and lose himself among the crowd of passengers making their way down the steps to the exit. If he hadn't already had a pressing appointment, he might have been tempted to follow him; he was bound to be up to no good. He rubbed his chin. He hoped Mace hadn't been 'associating with' Grady. Of course, they might have known each other from way back. They might have been in the same prison, even shared a cell, maybe, at some time. Angel wasn't looking for complications. It was his job to keep Grady alive, at least until after he'd given his evidence at Rikki Rossi's trial.

A tall, distinguished-looking man about thirty, in a suit as sharp as Maggie Thatcher's tongue, stepped down on to the platform from a following carriage. He had prematurely greying hair and a jet-black moustache. He was looking round. It was

47

Pete Grady all right. Angel recognised him from the photograph and discreetly waved the *Financial Times* to attract his attention. Grady spotted him. With his eyebrows raised, he advanced on Angel fast. He was carrying a suitcase in his left hand and had his right hand thrust hard down in his raincoat pocket. Angel didn't like that. He sensed danger. His jaw tightened. His pulse raced.

'You must be Michael Angel?' Grady said nonchalantly with the corners of his mouth turned upwards.

Angel didn't reply. He dropped the pink paper, closed in on the man, made a grab for his raincoat pocket with both hands, directed his hand towards the ground and squeezed very, very hard. As he suspected, through the gabardine he felt the barrel of a handgun.

Grady lost his cool.

'Get off!' he yelled and tried to batter him on the hip with the suitcase.

Several passengers rushing past gave them curious looks.

Grady lifted his knee to Angel's groin.

Angel anticipated it. He bent forward and stuck out his backside.

'You've got a gun!' Angel said, his jaw set like the Rock of Gibraltar. 'And that's not friendly.'

Grady didn't reply.

Angel squeezed his hand even harder.

'You're hurting, you fool,' Grady yelled. He stopped struggling.

'Take your hand out of your pocket . . . very slowly,' Angel said through his teeth while adjusting his grip so that Grady's fingers were free. 'Leave the gun in there.'

Grady's lips tightened. He brought out the crushed hand.

Angel dived into the pocket, pulled out the gun and glanced at it. It was a Walther PPK/S automatic. It was fully loaded with eight rounds. He checked the safety catch then pushed it into his own pocket.

Grady exercised his hand to recover the feeling. 'You can't take that iron. Angel. I need that. It's *me* they're looking for, you know.'

Angel glared at him.

'Come on,' he replied briskly. 'Let's go.'

He bent down, recovered the newspaper concealing the photograph, and walked briskly with the crowd down the steps, along the tunnel, up more steps to the ticket barrier, Grady keeping close behind. Once out of the station, they moved swiftly to his car which was on a yellow line at the front. Grady put his suitcase in the back and jumped into the front passenger seat. Angel raced up to the station traffic-lights as they turned red. He glared up at them and slammed on the brake.

'I want that iron back,' Grady snarled. 'There was nothing in the arrangement that said I couldn't carry a gun.'

Angel shook his head determinedly.

'I am a policeman, Grady. I can't let you swan around with a gun when I am un-armed. Stands to reason.'

The lights changed. Angel let in the clutch and turned left on to the North Bridge.

Grady rubbed his hand hard across his wet lips.

'Ask Strawbridge. Ring him up. He'll tell you. I don't think you appreciate the posi-tion I'm in,' he yelled.

Angel didn't reply. His jaw stiffened as he thought about it. But he was confident Strawbridge would agree with him that they couldn't let an ex-con walk about carrying a handgun while he hadn't so much as a peashooter to defend himself.

The car slowed. Grady looked out of the window. They were approaching a cross-roads. Angel turned left at the sign that read: Bromersley 12 m.

'Where are you putting me up then?'

'On your own, in a flat.'

Grady pursed his lips.

'Not a safe house?'

'No. The DS wasn't happy about the security. It's a small, self-contained furnished flat in a block of twelve. Near the centre of town. Rented from the council. Short term. Social Services. They think you are a charity case, needing temporary shelter while you recover from an illness. You couldn't be safer.'

'You mean they think I'm a tramp,' he growled.

'No. It's rather swish. You've got your own bed. Your own telly. Your own loo. Your own kitchen. I got Tesco to deliver a big shop this morning. All right?'

He wrinkled his nose.

'I could eat out.'

'You eat *there,*' Angel snapped.

'Mmm. No phone?'

Angel blinked.

'Who would you want to ring?'

'I got my mobile.'

'Don't use it, and don't answer it.'

'Who are the neighbours?'

'Mostly single, elderly retired folk. People on their own. You've just got to keep the door locked, and your face away from the window.'

He sniffed. 'Who knows about me, then?'

'Just the super and me. That's all. I tell you, you couldn't be safer.'

A mobile phone rang out; Angel dipped into his pocket, glanced at the LCD, then put it to his ear.

'Yes, sir? . . . . He's with me now. . . . Yes sir . . . straight to the flat . . . right, sir.'

He turned to Grady.

'He wants to speak to you.'

Grady's eyes lit up. He snatched the phone.

'Hey, Strawbridge, your man here has taken my gun. You know, I need a gun. If Rikki or Carl or Missis G or any of them get anywhere near me, I'm finished. You know that! They'll rub me out. Look, Strawbridge, if I'm going to do this for you, you've got to do this for me. I gotta have my protection with me, all the time, night and day, you promised me. And your man says you're not even putting me in a safe house . . . *I gotta have my gun.* . . . Yes. All right . . . all right. Hold on.'

He turned to Angel, grinned and passed him the phone.

Angel couldn't believe what was coming, and he didn't like it one bit. He put it to his ear.

'Angel . . . yes, sir. . . . yes, sir . . . yes, sir.'

He pulled a face like a man having his

prostate checked. He closed the phone, dropped it in his pocket. Then he drove on. He remained silent for a minute or so, then he took out the Walther and passed it to Grady.

Grady smiled and stuffed it into his raincoat pocket.

Angel drove into the service road at the back of Beckett's Flats. It was narrow and crammed with cars parked all down one side. He found a gap and managed to manoeuvre his way into it. As he switched off the ignition, he told Grady to stay in the car while he walked back to the narrow turning to see if anybody had been following them. He ran back to the corner, waited half a minute, it all seemed clear so he returned and together they made an orderly entrance through the back gate across the small yard and up three steps. He tapped a four digit code into the panel on the door. It was simple enough to remember. It was simply 4321. He saw that Grady had carefully watched him put in the number. The door opened. They climbed a flight of concrete steps with green painted iron railings round them, to a landing leading to a short corridor. They made for the last door on the left, number 12.

Angel took a keyring out of his pocket with two keys on it, threaded one off, shoved it in the door, unlocked it and waved to Grady to go in ahead of him. Then he withdrew the key, closed the door, put the key in the lock on the inside and locked it.

The door opened straight into the small freshly painted white sitting-room cum kitchen and Grady stood in the middle of it looking round at the big double window, the sink unit, the television set, the settee and the dining-table with two chairs. Everywhere was bright and clean, if a bit stark.

There were three doors leading out of the little room, and Angel stuck his head through each doorway in quick succession, checked the light switches and came back looking satisfied.

Grady watched him from the middle of the room. He sniffed.

'Like a pigeon loft.'

'You've been in worse,' Angel said, and he picked up the remote from the top of the television, and slumped down on a chair at the table. He switched the television on, looked round through the window at the main road and busy traffic outside and rubbed the lobe of his ear between his finger and thumb, wondering if he had forgotten anything. As the television came to life, he looked up at Grady and nodded at the set.

'Telly's working OK,' he announced brightly and turned it off.

Grady nodded, went into the bedroom, slung his suitcase on the bed, then mooched through the bathroom and loo doors, and poked in the cupboards and drawers, all the time muttering at everything he saw. Lastly, he spotted the bags of groceries on the kitchen worktop; he rushed over to them and pulled out a loaf of bread, some tins and packets and rummaged through the rest of the stuff. Eventually, he turned angrily to Angel and said, 'No booze!'

Angel glared up at him.

'You want to keep your wits about you, don't you?'

Grady put his hand to his mouth and began to nip and pull his bottom lip.

'You don't understand what it's like . . . what I'm going through. The risk I'm taking.'

Angel's face tightened then he rubbed his chin.

'It's only for a few days. You've just got to keep your head down and out of sight. There's a radio in the bedroom and there's the telly in here. There's plenty of grub. DS Strawbridge is calling later on today no doubt to check on you. Probably go through your deposition with you, that's all.'

'Well, it isn't all!' he suddenly snapped. 'There's more room in a tin of pilchards. And there's no back way out of here. If anybody comes to that door, there's no way out.'

'Who is going to come? Nobody knew you were coming up north, did they? Even if they did, we weren't followed from Doncaster, and we weren't followed in here, either. You couldn't be safer if you were in Fort Knox! *Nobody knows where you are!*'

'Carl and Mrs G and the rest of them will be out looking for me. They'll be looking and asking around all my usual places.'

'Well, you're not there, are you? They're wasting their time. They'll never find you here.'

Grady didn't reply. He turned away, slackened off his tie, took off his raincoat and dumped it over the chair.

'And there's the newspapers. They've got my picture. That *Daily Echo* man, Braddock, is a pain in the arse. They've got stringers, and people snooping all over the place.'

'You've nothing to worry about. Nobody saw you come in here. Just keep away from that window. They haven't got X-ray eyes. All right? I'll call in tomorrow. Try and relax. Watch the television or something.'

He ran his hand through his hair impatiently.

'I never watch television,' he lied. 'Have you got any cigarettes?'

Angel returned to the station and went straight down the corridor to Superintendent Strawbridge's office. He told him about Pete Grady and in particular repeated his concern about him possessing a loaded gun.

Strawbridge nodded.

'I have to get him in one piece to Manchester next Monday to testify against Ri'' i Rossi. If the cost of that is allowing him to carry a gun, then in these unusual and exceptional circumstances, I can live with it. I know he's been done in the past for possession, but there's no record that he's ever used it.'

'It's very risky, sir.'

'Well, what else can I do?'

'Take the gun off him and hope that he'll still co-operate,' Angel said bluntly.

'And if he doesn't?'

'He doesn't.'

Strawbridge's dark shadowy eyes narrowed. His lips tightened.

'Look here, Angel,' he began slowly, his voice chilling enough to frost up the inside

of a cell window. 'I've spent four years trying to get something on Rikki Rossi. Four
long years, and I'm not in the mood for let-
ting it all go down the pan for the sake of
bending a rule or two. He's probably the
most wanted man in the country. I have arrested him three times before, but the witnesses have always been murdered, disappeared or developed amnesia when I got
them into court. This time, I've got one. A
prize. One of his own gang. And he wants
to talk. He's eager to talk. I am going to do
everything in my power to get Grady into
court in one piece.'

Angel sighed.

Strawbridge continued.

'And I don't believe there's a risk, hardly
any risk at all.'

The phone rang. The superintendent
reached out for it.

'Strawbridge. . . . Right. . . . What's that
address again? . . . Got it. Tell them DI
Angel is on his way.'

He replaced the phone.

'There's a report of the murder of a man
at Frillies Country Club. Hotel Victor One
responded to a triple nine. Do you know
it?'

'Frillies? Yes sir. About two miles out of
town. On the Barnsley road. Never been

inside the place, though.'

'Now's your chance to widen your horizons. And by the way, there's a witness. Saw the whole thing, so it should be an easy one.'

Angel blinked. He stood up. He hoped Strawbridge was right. It was unusual to get an eyewitness.

'Right. Get on to it.'

Angel dashed out of the office. It was a relief. The further he was away from Strawbridge, Grady and the Rossis, the better he liked it. He charged up the corridor and saw Ahmed running towards him looking decidedly frantic and waving a sheet of A4.

'Sir. Sir,' he called urgently.

'What is it? Stuffing coming out of your teddy bear?' Angel growled while still pressing up the corridor.

'There's Mrs Buller-Price in reception to see you. She says it's very important,' Ahmed said trying to keep up the pace.

'Oh. I haven't time now. Give her my apologies, and be very polite. See if it's anything you can help her with. Or I'll see her tomorrow.'

'Right, sir.'

'But before that, phone SOCO, and tell him there's been a murder at Frillies Country Club. Then find DS Gawber and DS Crisp and tell them to join me there SAP.'

FOUR

Angel dashed out of the station to his car and pointed the bonnet out of the station yard. He had to concentrate on his driving to Frillies on Barnsley Road, as he was still smouldering over Grady having possession of a gun. His mind shot like an arrow to the picture of himself earlier that day in the car actually handing back the loaded Walther (probably stolen, at that!) to a beaming Peter Grady. He couldn't believe what he had done. And he could still see the smug expression on the man's suntanned face, the gleam of triumph in his eye, as he had snatched it out of his hand and slipped it triumphantly into his pocket. He couldn't blank out the scene. He must have been mad!

A car horn blared aggressively behind.

He looked up at the traffic lights; they had turned green. He let in the clutch, turned left into Barnsley Road, straightened up the wheel, changed gear and checked the traffic behind in his mirror, then passed a Yorkshire Traction bus. He couldn't be far from Frillies.

He rubbed his chin and blew out a long sigh. Strawbridge's ruling allowing Grady to carry the Walther was definitely not a measured, professional decision. If the chief constable had known he would have gone doolally! Angel understood well enough the need to get Rikki Rossi locked away; he could sympathize with Strawbridge's predicament, but he was against permitting Grady to have a gun. You can never allow a villain to be armed! It's not on. It's not safe. He'd seen the horrific damage a gun could do. Many, many times. The sickening sights he had seen. Gunshot wounds to the head or chest were almost always fatal. The funerals he had attended. The grief he'd witnessed. Wherever a crook had a gun, death surely followed.

He changed up to top gear.

And yet when a station policeman wanted to draw a gun, what a to-do! Huh! There was a very strict procedure governing it all; rules and regulations a mile long; signatures, witnesses; counting the rounds on issue; justifying every one fired; and careful accounting for the live ammo handed back in

61

when the incident was over. A policeman should never have to approach a criminal known to be armed, without being armed himself.

A red traffic-light ahead needed his full attention. He slowed down. It changed to green, he changed back up, went over the crossroads and realized he was almost at the Country Club. On the right was a high stone wall. He travelled alongside it for two hundred yards until he came to large wooden gates, which were open and fastened back. He read the smartly painted signs, white on black, fastened to the walls. They said: 'Frillies Country Club. Private. Members only.'

That's where he had to be. He tapped the indicator stalk, and drove through the gates on to a long tarmacadam drive which cut through lawns, trees, evergreen bushes and shrubs eventually to reveal a large imposing stone-built house that appeared to have previously been the residence of a wealthy Victorian family. He drove under the pillared portico and beyond and parked behind a white van he recognized to be that of one of the SOCO teams. A young uniformed PC on duty saw him drive up and dashed through the front door to meet him.

'Oh. It's you, sir,' he said, throwing up a salute.

'Yes. It's Grainger, isn't it? What's happened?' Angel said, as they walked briskly together towards the entrance.

'We answered a triple nine, sir. A man's dead. Stabbed. The club manager told us there'd been an accident. There is a witness: a young woman, in a bit of a state.'

Angel wrinkled his nose.

'Show me. The crime scene first.'

PC Grainger led Angel across the thick, well-trodden carpet in front of the reception counter, past the lift doors, down an oak-panelled corridor with aspidistras in pots on dark wooden stands positioned intermittently on both sides, to some glass doors at the end. The doors, with graciously ornate brass handles, were wedged open, and there was a hand painted copperplate sign on the arch above, that read: 'Conservatory'.

'In there, sir,' Grainger said with a flick of a thumb.

Angel peered through the door, but didn't go in.

The glass, high-roofed room with huge windows was overloaded with evergreen plants, in pots, on stands and on the floor, mostly placed round the perimeter of the room. The furniture comprised twenty or more easy chairs, a settee, and a black, grand piano with matching stool. The grey, mottled, mastic floor was covered in plastic sheeting all the way from the door up to the middle of the room where the figure of a man lay on his face in a pool of blood.

At the far side of the room, the backs of two men in white paper suits, plastic hats and white rubber boots appeared incongruously through the foliage. They were bending forward looking down at the floor. They heard Angel and Grainger and turned back to face them.

'This should be taped up,' Angel bawled, indicating the open doorway.

The older one said. 'Yes, sir. Next job. We've only been here two minutes. I'm DS Taylor.'

'I know who you are. What have you got?'

'Not much, sir,' Taylor said. He pointed to the corpse. 'Young man in his twenties. One stab wound only, I think, in the heart or aorta. There's a witness in a room along the corridor, sir. A young woman.'

'I'll see the witness while you get organized. Get that tape up.'

'Right, sir,' Taylor waved in acknowledgment.

Angel turned to Grainger.

64

'This way, sir.'

He turned round and directed him to a door on his left, next to the conservatory. It had the words: 'Reading Room', painted above it.

'In there, sir.'

Angel nodded and said, 'Right. You'd better get back to the front door.'

Grainger nodded, turned away and went down the corridor.

Angel knocked on the door of the Reading Room, opened it and went inside. It was a small room with just a few easy chairs and a writing desk against the far wall. There was a pretty young woman sitting forward on an easy chair holding her head in her hands, her legs drawn up tightly underneath her. She had a handkerchief on her lap. She didn't look up. A young man in his twenties, in a well-cut dark suit and red tie, sitting next to her, looked across at the door. His face brightened as he saw Angel approach.

'Are you the police?' he said, rising to his feet.

'Inspector Angel. Who are you?'

'Martin Tickell. I'm the club manager,' he said. He then turned towards the young lady. 'It was this lady who came here with Mr Schumaker, the dead man, as his guest, a member . . . the man who was stabbed. Erm. She's not very talkative. If you'll excuse me, I've some things I must see to. I'll be in the office, if you want me, inspector.'

Angel nodded and looked down at the girl.

Tickell rushed out of the door, glad to be away.

She looked up. She was only young, eighteen or nineteen years, her fresh, pretty face spoiled by her red eyes and wet cheeks.

Angel took his time. He dug into his pocket and pulled out his mobile phone. He tapped in a number.

Ahmed answered.

'Yes, sir?'

'Ahmed. I am at Frillies Country Club. Get Sergeant Hollis to let me have a WPC to assist me here, urgently. Tell her to come to the reading room to attend a witness and stay with her. Got it?'

'Right, sir.'

He closed the phone and stuffed it back into his pocket. Then he looked round the little room. It had two writing bureaux at one end and twenty or so easy chairs in chintz designs arranged around small coffee tables in groups of four or five.

He moved to the comfortable-looking chair opposite her, eased himself into it, rubbed his chin, then in a soft, quiet voice, said, 'Can you talk, miss? Are you up to it yet?'

She sniffed then nodded.

'I'm the policeman investigating this case. Perhaps you could tell me what happened? You could start by telling me your name.'

'My name is Eloise Macdonald.'

'And what actually happened, Eloise?'

She was slow to start speaking. 'It was awful. Oh it was awful. We were sat on the settee in the . . . the conservatory. Talking . . .'

'Yes,' Angel said encouragingly.

'Oh,' she sighed. 'Just talking . . .'

'Who was there?'

'My boyfriend, Richard. We had just had a lovely meal. I shall never forget it. We were going to have coffee . . . it was wonderful . . . the only man I shall ever love . . .' her voice trailed away.

She struck a sympathetic chord with Angel. He didn't want to rush her.

'And what happened?'

'We were talking; it was beautiful. He was a lovely man . . . I was just getting to know him, then it was . . . ruined. The door suddenly opened and what I believe was a tin can, an empty beer can, something like that, came flying into the room and landed just in front of us, at our feet. I looked at the door, and a man in a black T-shirt and jeans, and wearing a mask, leaped into the room. He had a long knife in his hand, like a kitchen knife. He came up to Richard and stood in front of the settee and sort of . . . challenged him. He said something like, "Your time is up. That girl is mine," meaning me. Richard didn't know what he was talking about and said "What do you want?" Then he looked at me. Well, I didn't know the man either. Never seen him before in my life as far as I know. Couldn't see his face, of course.'

'Yes,' Angel said. 'A mask. What sort of a mask? What was it made of, Eloise? Paper?'

'It was all black. Looked like some sort of cardboard. It was held on by elastic round the back of his head. Anyway, I heard Richard say to him, "Why the mask?" '

'And what did he say?'

'He didn't reply.'

Angel shook his head.

'What happened next?'

'I told him that I didn't know him, and asked him to leave us alone. He laughed, like a sneer. He looked back at me and said something like, "That woman's mine." It was awful. Richard faced him sort of square on. Then the man came up to him and began stabbing the air with the knife. Richard looked round for something to defend himself with, or hit him with or something. There was nothing. I was terrified. I think I screamed. I went behind the settee. Richard dodged his attacks, then suddenly he turned, dragged one of the cushions from the settee, used it as a shield to push against him. The man reached out to try to grab hold of it, but didn't get a good enough grip. Richard then threw it into his face. Then he made a grab for his wrist — the one holding the knife. He managed to get hold of it with both hands and he squeezed it and squeezed it. The man kept hitting him on the head with his free hand. It was obviously hurting Richard, but he hung on. Eventually, both men landed on the floor. It was frightening. Richard still kept hold of his wrist and banged his hand repeatedly on the hard floor several times and told him to drop the knife. Eventually he did. Then Richard reached out, snatched it up, put his knee on the man's chest and held the knife to his throat. I thought he was going to kill him, but he didn't. He told the man to get up, and he pulled him up by his shirt. They reached their feet. They were both panting and red in the face. Richard released his grip on the man to straighten his coat and adjust his coat and tie. Then, suddenly, the man reached out, snatched the knife out of Richard's hand and pushed it hard into his chest. Blood spurted out immediately. Oh, it was terrible. Terrible . . .'

She had to stop. She looked down. Her shoulders began to shake.

Angel leaned back in the chair and waited.

After a minute or so, she took a deep breath and said, 'There was blood all over. Richard gasped, reached for his chest, looked up into the man's face then collapsed in front of the settee. I think I fainted. I had had a few glasses of wine. Anyway, I don't quite know what happened then. When I woke up, the club manager was shaking my shoulders. I thought at first it was all a horrible dream. Then I saw Richard on the floor at my feet and I knew it wasn't.'

She sobbed a little while.

Angel took out his leather-backed notebook and wrote something rapidly.

Then she looked up. 'Are you. . . . a policeman?'

'Inspector Angel. Now, what was the name of the — your young man, and where did he live?'

'I don't know where he lived . . . round here somewhere. He said his house wasn't far away. His name was Richard

Schumaker.'

'And had you known him long?'

'A week, only, Inspector.'

'Mmm. And can you give me a description of the man who attacked him?'

'Mmm. Tall. Dark hair. Tight jeans. Black T-shirt. I told you about the mask: it was frightening. It covered his eyes, forehead and cheeks, right down to the chin, holes cut in it for the eyes and mouth, of course.'

'Was he wearing gloves?'

'No.'

'But you couldn't see anything unusual about him, his hair, his arms, his hands?'

'Yes. He had a tattoo of a skull and crossbones on the back of his left hand, in blue.'

There was a knock at the door.

Angel was not pleased. He screwed up his face.

'Excuse me,' he said, and crossed to the door and opened it ten inches.

It was Gawber.

'I was told you were in here, sir.'

'Yes. Where's Crisp?'

'Don't know, sir.'

'Never mind. A young man's been murdered in the conservatory, Richard Schumaker, over there. Check on all the access points to this building, see if any is covered by CCTV. Looking for a tall man, brown hair, jeans, black T-shirt, in his twenties, tattoo on his left hand. He'll be well covered in blood.'

'I need to see you now, Mr Tickell?' Angel said across the reception desk, which was a small counter by the main door of the club.

'Yes, of course,' the smart young man replied. 'You're Inspector Angel, didn't you say? Come into the office,' he said, pointing at a mahogany veneered door to the side. 'We can talk in there. It's more private and more comfortable.'

'Thank you,' Angel said.

Tickell disappeared through an arch at the back of the area and reappeared at the side door.

Angel stepped into the small, tidy little room.

Tickell pointed to a comfortable-looking balloon-backed chair.

'Please sit down, inspector,' he said and he took an old wooden swivel chair behind the desk. 'I've never had anything like this to deal with, inspector. And believe me, as secretary of the club all sorts of different situations and problems crop up from time to time.'

Angel nodded understandingly and took the opportunity to glance at the back of the man's left hand for the tattoo of a skull and crossbones, but the hand was clean.

'A few questions. Won't take long. I want to see everybody who was in the building at the time of the murder.'

'There was only Walter the chef, Louis the waiter and me.'

Angel made a note of the names in his book. He raised his eyebrows and said: 'Nobody else, other members, customers?'

'We've been tremendously busy over the festive season, Inspector, and we'll be very busy tonight. There's a limit to how much enjoyment our members can tolerate,' he said wryly. 'But we are not usually busy in the daytime, however, a lot of members working and so on. Some Fridays and at weekends, it will be very busy for lunches and so on then.'

Tickell picked up a printed card A6 size and glanced at it. 'This is the membership card of Richard Schumaker. I looked this out. He hasn't been a member long. Applied to join in October. He was accepted on the nod by the committee at the early November meeting, as nobody knew anything about him. He gave his address as The Brambles, Harrogate Road, Clarendon, Bromersley. It's only a cockstride out of our front gate. He didn't fill in the employment box. I've no idea what he did for a living. He gave his age at 25.'

'Right. Well, tell me all that you can about him and his young lady, Eloise Macdonald and, in particular, what happened today.'

'There's little to tell,' Martin Tickell replied. 'He applied in person, I recall, to be a member. Polite, well-spoken young man. Nothing remarkable about that. I believe he has been here for lunch once before with a guest.'

'The young lady, he brought with him today?'

'I'm not sure.'

Angel wrinkled his nose. 'Could be important.'

'I don't remember. So many people, you know.'

Angel sighed. 'What do you remember about him?'

'Nothing. Sorry.'

'Did he speak to any other members or the staff, or anybody?'

'Didn't notice, Inspector. There are a lot of comings and goings, over six hundred members, you know. Louis might know or some of the other staff.'

'Mmm. Did he make a reservation in advance for today?'

'He phoned in. On Friday, I think. Simply

74

asked to book a table for two, himself and a guest. I said it was fine and he duly arrived with the young lady. He signed the book; they left their coats in the cloakroom and went into the bar. I didn't see any more of them until I was passing the conservatory door at about two-thirty or so, looked in and saw a figure on the floor and the young woman apparently in a faint or something, slumped on the sofa.'

Tickell's forehead became moist. He took out a handkerchief and began to pat it. He licked his lips.

'I went into the room. There was a pool of blood . . . it was dreadful, Inspector, I can tell you, and the young woman, Eloise Macdonald was . . . her eyes were closed. I took her by the shoulders and was going to shake her. Her eyes opened. She looked at me, then at the floor at. . . . and began to cry. I asked her what had happened; she just looked at member Schumaker and cried. My first thought was an ambulance, so I dashed back here and dialled 999. The lady on the phone suggested that the police should be informed. I agreed. Then I ran back down to the conservatory. The young woman was where I had left her, I suggested we move out. I helped her into the Reading Room and stayed with her until your men

75

arrived . . . and — that's about it.'

Angel pursed his lips.

'Thanks very much. That'll do for now. I need to see Walter the chef, and Louis the waiter. Will you organise that for me? Can I see them here? One at a time, privately.'

'Of course. Yes,' he said most courteously and reached out for the phone.

A young man, about 25, kitted out in whites and a chef's hat came into the office. 'You wanted to see me? I heard about the dead man in the conservatory. I suppose it's murder.'

Angel nodded and closed the door.

'Please sit down. I am Inspector Angel. Won't keep you long. What is your name?'

'Walter Flagg.'

'Worked here long, Mr Flagg?'

'Two years now. Shortly after I finished training.'

Angel glanced down to the back of the man's left hand. He wasn't surprised to note that there was no tattoo of a skull and cross-bones.

'Did you know the dead man, the new member, Richard Schumaker?'

'No, Inspector. I work in the kitchens, rarely get out into club rooms. Maybe I get a peep into the restaurant once in a while. I am very much a backroom boy.'

'You cooked the meal he and the young lady with him ate at lunchtime today. Notice anything unusual about them or the meal?'

'No. They were the only customers today for lunch. It's not usually so slack, but it's just after the holidays. Christmas, New Year, everybody is just sick of food, aren't they? Busy tonight, though.'

'Did you see anything of a tall young man, wearing a mask, with a tattoo on the back of his hand, carrying a knife, this afternoon or anytime today?'

Flagg frowned, shook his head and said, 'No, Inspector.'

'Didn't come taking a short cut through the kitchen?'

'No. Definitely not.'

'You saw nothing of a stranger like that, or a man you didn't know wearing other clothes?'

'No, Inspector. There's been nobody in the kitchen today apart from Mr Tickell earlier and then Louis, who was waiting on the member and his guest . . . sorry.'

Angel sniffed.

'You're not missing a knife, are you?'

'A knife?'

Walter Flagg frowned, then his jaw dropped. He shook his head thoughtfully.

'You mean the weapon that . . . I don't know, Inspector. There are lots of knives in the kitchen. If one was missing, I wouldn't know. I'm sorry.'

Angel nodded.

'Thank you, Mr Flagg.'

'I am Louis Dingle. You wanted to see me, sir?'

Angel nodded, pulled out his notebook and made a note of the young man's name.

'Yes. Please come in. Sit down.'

The handsome young man dressed immaculately in tails, starched shirt-front and dickie bow came in, closed the door and sat down.

Angel pursed his lips and glanced down at the back of the man's hand for a tattoo, but it was as plain and pink as a policeman's expense chitty.

'Nice people,' Dingle said. 'I don't know what could have happened in there in the conservatory. They were all right when I saw them out of the restaurant.'

'No problems, nothing unusual over lunch, Mr Dingle?'

'No. They had booked a table for 12 noon. They were on time. Went straight in the bar. Had a couple of drinks and then ordered *à la carte*. I left them chatting until their

78

starter was ready. Then I showed them through into the restaurant. They took their time over the meal. Seemed to enjoy it. They didn't have coffee. They said they might have it later in the conservatory. They left; I held the door open. We weren't busy so I took the dirty pots through to the kitchen and had a cup of tea with Walter — he's the duty chef. I went back to the restaurant, and tidied round. Then I went into the bar, rinsed the glasses. Returned to the restaurant, began to set the rest of the tables for this evening. Then two men in police uniforms and dayglo coats came into the bar. They asked me where the dead man was. I didn't know what they were talking about. I was curious. They went out. I followed them across the hall to the conservatory. The door was open. I could see the member on the floor.'

'You didn't go in?'

'No. No,' he said, shaking his head. 'I didn't want to. I went straight down to the chef, Walter, and told him. We were both very shocked.'

'Have you noticed if there is a knife missing? The man was stabbed. . . .'

'No. Not from the dining-room,' he said quickly. 'Not as far as I know.'

'Did you happen to overhear any of the

conversation between them?'

'No. They were both quietly spoken, almost in whispers. I expect they were a courting couple, looked at each other a lot. He was over the top with courtesy and generosity; if she had wanted champagne, I reckon he would have bought her a vineyard!'

'Did you see anything of another man, or anybody else for that matter, in the dining-room or the bar or the hall, or anywhere at all?'

'No.'

'The man I am looking for was wearing a mask. He had a tattoo on the back of his hand, carrying a knife. Did you see anybody at all this afternoon or anytime today?'

'I didn't see anybody at all, Inspector, except Mr Tickell, Walter Flagg and the two customers, until the police arrived.'

'Then what happened?'

'I was in the kitchen. The bell went in the reading room. I answered it. It was Mr Tick-ell wanting some tea for the young lady. I made it quickly and took it in. She was in a state.'

'Thank you, Mr Dingle.'

Angel came out of Tickell's office and closed the door just as a clock chimed. He looked round. It was the big grandfather in the hall by the reception desk. It said 6.15. He must remember to ring his wife Mary, as soon as he could. She would be wondering where he was. His tea would be spoiling. He made his way determinedly along the panelled corridor, past the snooker-room door to the reading room.

Eloise Macdonald was still in there, in the same chair, now appearing to be alert and composed. WPC Leisha Baverstock had arrived and was sitting opposite her. She was looking at her, appropriately attentive.

She stood up when Angel entered.

He was pleased to see her there. He waved her to sit down and said, 'You're on overtime.'

She smiled slightly.

'That's all right, sir.'

He nodded.

Eloise Macdonald said, 'I must go home, inspector.' She looked at her hands and opened them to expose the palms. 'And clean up. Look at me. And my mother will wonder where I am.'

Angel sat down in the chair between the two young women. He looked at Eloise and leaned forward. 'Feeling better?'

She nodded and smiled wanly.

'Good. Good. Just a couple of questions.

Won't keep you long. How long did you know Richard Schumaker?'

'Oh? A week or so,' she said hesitating. 'This was our first date. But I had noticed him before, many times. He comes in . . . came into the place where I work. Every week. I am the cashier at Cheapos super-market. I have seen him at checkouts many a time, when I have been going down the tills. He used to look at me and smile, friendly like, and whistle. He was absolutely wonderful. I hardly knew him at all. We got chatting over a coffee in the café, last Friday. He asked me when I got my day off. This week it was Monday, so he said would I like to come out for lunch. I agreed, so he sent a car for me, and met me here.'

Angel frowned.

'Sent a car for you? Where does he work? What does he do?'

Eloise's mouth dropped open. She looked first at Leisha Baverstock and then at Angel.

'I . . . er. I thought you would know him. He's sort of . . . in your line of work.'

Angel shook his head.

'He works undercover. He liaises between Interpol and the police,' she said. Suddenly, her expression changed to one of puzzle-ment. 'He said he knew all the local police, from the chief constable downwards, and they knew him! But that you were instructed not to acknowledge each other in public. In fact the car he sent to pick me up was a police car camouflaged to look like a taxi.'

Angel frowned. He pursed his lips. There were lots of new channels of communication affecting domestic and overseas security these days between the UK police, MI5, MI6, Special Branch, Scotland Yard, the Home Office and Interpol, that were above Angel's head, but a young man allocated a police car, and a driver, camouflaged to look like a taxi cab and directed to collect a girlfriend on a social trip? No.

'I believe he was . . . pulling your leg, Eloise.'

Her mouth opened wide.

'Certainly not,' she said strongly. 'He swore me to secrecy, Inspector.'

Angel noticed a change in her expression. Her eyes moved thoughtfully from side to side. She was clearly uncomfortable with the situation.

'I'd better not say any more,' she said firmly.

Angel's eyes narrowed.

'We've got to find who murdered him, Eloise. Whatever information you might have may be vital. Anything that may provide a lead to his killer must come before any promise you might have made to him when he was alive.'

She shook her head firmly.

'No,' she said stubbornly. 'I must go home.'

Angel licked his lips. He looked into her eyes.

'It is absolutely imperative that —'

'No,' she interrupted. 'I must go home.' She closed her handbag, grabbed the strap and stood up. 'I must go home. I have nothing more to say, and I refuse to be held here any longer against my will.'

Angel's eyebrows shot up.

'You're not being held against your will. In fact, you can leave whenever you want. WPC Baverstock will take you home, won't you?'

The policewoman stood up.

Eloise made for the door.

Leisha Baverstock looked back at Angel, her eyebrows raised.

He nodded approvingly and waved an encouraging hand.

'Goodnight, Eloise,' he said. 'I'll see you tomorrow.'

She looked back, her face looked very troubled; she was about to say something, changed her mind and went out. Leisha Baverstock followed and closed the door.

Angel leaned back in the chair, blew out a long sigh and rubbed his chin.

FIVE

'What is it?'

'There's Mrs Buller-Price here again,' Ahmed said. 'She's very anxious to see you, sir. She's in reception. And DS Gawber's here.'

Angel looked up at the door and saw the sergeant with a file of papers standing patiently next to the cadet.

'Come in, Ron.'

'Good morning, sir.'

'Aye, good morning. Sit down. Wait a couple of minutes, Ahmed, and then show her in here.'

The cadet nodded and closed the door.

Gawber took the seat by Angel's desk.

'Yes, Ron?'

'Nothing suspicious in the club itself, sir,' Gawber said. 'With Mr Tickell's help, I recovered Schumaker's overcoat from the cloakroom and passed it on to SOCO, but there doesn't seem to be anything unusual about it.'

'No. Right. Anything else?'

'I've got six men still combing the grounds. Nothing turned up as yet.'

'Hmmm. I interviewed the manager, a cook and a waiter cum bartender. They each say they saw nothing, and none had a tattoo on the back of his hand. Surprisingly, those were the only people in the club apart from the victim and Eloise Macdonald.'

'Hmmm. Have another go at that manager, Tickell. See if anything apparently unrelated but unusual occurred yesterday. Anything stolen, misplaced, missing; you know what I mean.'

Gawber rubbed his chin.

'There was one thing, sir. I don't suppose it's relevant: while I was with Mr Tickell, a man came in with an overcoat, a member, said he'd taken it by mistake the night previously, full of apologies, didn't realize until he got home that it wasn't his. Mr Tickell told him that another member had earlier complained that his coat had gone missing also, and that he had had to go home without a coat. It was freezing too. They had obviously taken each other's by mistake. Tickell said it happened all the time. It usually sorted itself out the following day. However the man went to the cloakroom while I was there, said he couldn't find his own coat.'

Angel frowned.

'Ah. So the man's coat had not been brought back.'

'That's right, sir.'

There was a knock at the door.

'Come in,' Angel called.

It was Ahmed.

'Just a moment,' Angel said, and turned back to Gawber. 'Ron, you'd better nip back to the club straight away, follow up that missing coat. Get a full description of it. It might be important.'

Gawber nodded and left quickly.

Angel then turned to Ahmed.

'Right,' he said. 'Show her in.'

Mrs Buller-Price bustled into the office.

'Thank you,' she said to Ahmed, who smiled politely and left, quietly closing the door.

'Sorry to keep you waiting, Mrs Buller-Price.'

'Ah, now there you are, inspector. I came yesterday but was told you were out. I can see that you are busy,' she said. 'I am so sorry to add to your burden. Oh dear!'

Angel smiled.

'Do sit down, and tell me how can I help you?'

'Dear Inspector Angel. Thank you,' she said panting. She flopped in the leather chair by his desk, put her heavy walking stick on the floor on one side, dragged the big leather bag on to her ample knees, dug around inside it, pulled out a brown envelope, lowered the bag to the floor, adjusted her waterproof hat, which had gone askew in the business of settling down, and then turned to face him. She pursed her lips, then holding the envelope firmly, she put on a cherubic smile and began.

'Well, Inspector, it's like this, and I do hope you can help me. Oh dear. Early yesterday morning, I had a strange telephone call from a man. He said, as near as I can remember, that a car had come up in the night, that it had been put in the barn for me, that I was to try it out for a month or two and that it was mine to use and that I would be under no obligation. Well, I was astonished at this, of course, but before I could tell him that I couldn't possibly afford to buy a new car, and that he'd better take it back straightaway, he'd put the receiver down.'

Angel looked at her and smiled. He had to concede this was somewhat unusual.

'Well now,' she continued. 'There were some keys pushed through the letterbox, so

I took them out to the barn and discovered the most beautiful new car you have ever seen. Now, Inspector, I have not shown any interest in purchasing a new car from anybody. I have not even made an enquiry about a car by post or telephone or in any other way. This car has come completely out of the blue. Although it is true that my Bentley is temporarily out of commission, I am *not* in the market for a car and I certainly could not afford one in this price range. It must be returned. The question is, to whom? Anyway, on the driver's seat was this envelope.'

She placed it firmly in front of him.

He picked it up. It was unsealed. Inside were the new vehicle registration document and a fully comprehensive insurance certificate for the car; both were made out in the name of Mrs Alicia Buller-Price.

Angel glanced at them, looked up at her and said, 'I think we may be able to find out where the car came from.'

She beamed at him.

'Where is the car now?'

'Outside the front of the station, Inspector. I have brought it for you to see. I have been driving it around all day. Getting used to it. It's a magnificent car. I hope that that's all right?'

'Hmmm. The insurance looks satisfactory, and it is a brand new vehicle. It must be roadworthy. Doesn't need an MOT.'

'Oh yes,' she said proudly. 'Only forty-two miles on the clock. I do hope you can solve the mystery for me and, even if you cannot, at least you might be able to advise where I can return it, or have it collected or . . .'

'Don't worry any more about it. Leave these documents with me. I'll look into it and I'll give you a ring as soon as I can.'

'That's very kind,' she said with another big cherubic smile.

'Not at all, Mrs Buller-Price. I am very pleased to be able to help.'

She pursed her lips, looked at him, then fingered the big cameo on the gold chain round her neck and said, 'It is all right for me to keep driving it around? I wouldn't want to do anything illegal.'

'Drive it to the end of the earth, if you wish,' he said rising to his feet. 'In the meantime, I'll look into it and let you know.'

'Thank you.'

She gave him a big broad smile, leaned down for her stick and bag and stood up looking round the office.

'Do you know this room is painted the same colour as the Archbishop of Canterbury's dressing-room.'

'Oh really?' he said politely. He was never really surprised at anything Mrs Buller-Price said.

'Yes. Delightful apple green.'

He smiled, went to the door and opened it.

'I'll get Ahmed to show you out.'

'Come in. Come in,' Angel bawled. 'I've been looking for you all over the place. Where have you been? Potholing? Don't bother. It's bound to be somewhere I can't check up on!'

DS Crisp stood by the door his hand on the knob.

'Well, are you coming in or not?'

'Oh,' he said. 'Yes. Right, sir.'

He closed the door and approached Angel's desk.

'I've been very busy, sir.'

Angel shook his head impatiently.

'Well, doing what? I'm listening.'

'I'm on that misper, sir. That 22-year-old model, missing since early December. Tania Pulman.'

'Tania Pulman? Oh yes.'

Angel knew of the case. Very worrying. He'd had the photograph and description. Local girl, doing well for herself. Disappeared off the face of the earth. The parents distraught.

'Foul play?' he asked.

'Still uncertain, sir.'

'Boyfriends? Ex-boyfriends? Neighbours? Sugar daddies?'

'Been through them all.'

'Advised all channels, the Salvation Army?'

'Yes, sir.'

'Right, well you can leave it for now,' he said, and swivelled round to a wire basket on the table behind his desk. He picked up a videotape and thrust it out to him. 'I've brought a CCTV tape from Frillies Country Club, the scene of a murder. It only covers the front entrance. I am looking for a tall, young man, in his twenties, in jeans, black T-shirt, in a mask, with a tattoo of a skull and crossbones on the back of his left hand, possibly carrying a long knife of some sort!'

Crisp grinned.

'Is this a halloween prank, sir?'

Angel stared at him with a face as straight as a copper's asp.

'No. It's for real!' he snapped. 'That's what our witness said she saw. I want you to spin through it smartly, note all possible candidates, the time of their arrival and the time they leave. And I want to know who they are; obviously, the murderer is hardly likely to be wearing all that gear, the mask and so forth when he —'

There was a knock at the door.

Angel said irritably, 'See who that is.'

Crisp opened the door.

Ahmed and Eloise Macdonald were standing there.

'Oh yes. Ah, come in, Eloise. Won't keep you a minute. Thank you, Ahmed,' Angel said, and he turned back to Crisp. 'Have you got all that? You can liaise with the manager at the club; he should be able to supply names and addresses.'

'Yes, sir.'

'Right. Crack on, then.'

Crisp went out and closed the door.

Angel smiled at the young woman and pointed to the chair.

'Good morning, Eloise. Did you sleep all right?'

'It took a little while, but once I got off, I slept through all right,' she replied, quietly settling into the chair.

'Good. Good.'

'I feel a bit silly, Inspector,' she began tentatively. 'I mean, you really are a police inspector, and this is a police station.'

He nodded.

'And I thought he was so wonderful. You know, there was a time last night when I

94

thought you weren't the police.'

'Well, who did you think we were?'

'I don't know: a foreign power, spies. It was Richard, Richard Schumaker. He told me some outrageous lies, Inspector. I've been thinking about it. What a fool I've been. He said that he was a senior officer in MI6 and that he was working under cover; that the country club was the secret meeting place for some far eastern fascist organization that he had to infiltrate and break up. I see now that it was all rubbish. And that police car was disguised to look like a taxi! How ridiculous I must have looked to you.'

Angel thoughtfully shook his head. 'It was simply a taxi that he'd booked and paid for in advance, that's all,' he said. 'It's a common ploy to impress young ladies.'

She nodded, not a little sadly.

'Why would he do that?'

'Makes him feel big, important. Or, I have another theory about that. Anyway, as long as you are now sure about who are the good guys?'

She smiled wanly and nodded.

'Eloise, I want to know what he *really* did for a living?'

'I don't know, Inspector. As I said, I really believed he worked for MI6.'

'Well I can assure you, he doesn't. Early this morning, my chief contacted the very top, informed them that Richard Schumaker was dead, telegraphed a post-mortem photograph of him and MI6 has categorically declared that they've never heard of him and that they've no interest in him. They couldn't have been more negative.'

She lowered her head and shook it a little.

'I am sorry,' Angel said gently. 'I can only say that you've been duped by an experienced liar.'

She sighed.

'Tell me, Eloise,' he continued, 'Is it possible that you had a boyfriend, lover, whatever, that sought revenge and he chose to punish you by murdering Richard Schumaker before your eyes? You said he was wearing a full face mask; behind the mask, could it have been someone that you know?'

'No, Inspector. I don't think it's anybody I know.'

'You said that he said, "That girl is mine." What did it mean?'

'I don't know. But I know that I have never had a boyfriend as tall as that man . . . excepting Richard, of course. They were about the same height.'

Angel sighed.

'Now, you said your job was that of cash-

96

ier; I suppose you handle a lot of cash?'

'Yes. I do. Thousands of pounds. *Many* thousands of pounds.'

'What exactly do you do?'

'Well, as the tills fill up with cash, I go down them, all twenty-two, periodically, take the excess paper money, leave a chitty, then wrap it, bag it, and shoot it into the day safe. Then later, when each girl cashes in, I reconcile the excess with their till rolls. Also, I prepare it, load it into bags for the security firm to collect.'

Angel's jaw stiffened as he rubbed it.

'Maybe he was lining you up for some sort of a con. He didn't let drop any names of any friends, or anybody at all, did he?'

'No. Only . . . he said his father was a surgeon.'

'Oh? Whereabouts?'

'Didn't say.'

'Hmmm. I'll look into that.'

He pulled out the notebook and scratched a note in it.

'The man that killed Schumaker, he couldn't have been an ex-boyfriend. He couldn't have been a jealous lover that you separated from.'

She smiled briefly. The thought had somehow amused her. She sighed, shook her head and then looked down to hide her sad eyes.

Angel noticed and desperately tried to think of something kind to say.

'Right, Eloise. I think that's all for now. Sorry that you've been cruelly tricked like this.'

'Come in. What have you got?'

DS Gawber closed the door.

Angel pointed to the chair by the desk.

'That coat has not been returned, sir. It's a fair guess it was taken by the murderer. It's just an ordinary grey raincoat. Bought off the peg from Challender's.'

'It won't be that ordinary, the prices they charge,' Angel said. 'It'll presumably have their label in the back of the neck.'

'And the owner said he had left a pair of yellow woollen gloves in the pockets.'

'Yes. Right,' Angel said. He made a note on the back of an envelope. 'Anything else?'

'Yes, sir. Following up the search for his next-of-kin, there isn't a doctor or a surgeon in South Yorkshire called Schumaker, sir. He's not on any NHS, GP or hospital list, or any other list. So I phoned through to the BMA. They had a Haydn Schumaker in Liverpool, a plastic surgeon, but they have no current address for him; he's been out of

98

touch for two years. They don't get any reply from him at his last known address, which was The Elms, Wallasey Road.'

'Mmm. That lass, Eloise Macdonald didn't even know the lad's address. I got it from Martin Tickle from his Frillies membership application. We need to look over his place urgently.'

Gawber started grinning.

'Just thought, sir. A plastic surgeon, the girl said,' he grinned. 'I suppose that means he fixes up these models with bigger . . . bosoms and —'

'Yeah. Yeah,' Angel interrupted quickly.

'Must be in the money, then.'

'Get over to his house. Might be a lead staring us in the face.'

Gawber stood up to leave.

Angel pursed his lips, reached out for the phone and said, 'Hang on a minute. I'll just make this call and then I'll come along with you.'

He dialled a number.

'Right, sir,' Gawber said, returning to the seat.

'I'll see if I can get any joy from Liverpool. If this chap's in the plastic surgery racket, he'd need his clients to be able to get easy access to him. He shouldn't be difficult to find.'

A chirpy Liverpudlian woman soon answered: 'Liverpool central, CID.'

'Yes. DI Angel, Bromersley CID. Can I speak to the duty officer, please?'

'Hold on, sir,' the woman said.

There were a few clicks and then a man's voice said, 'DI Callahan, duty officer. What can I do for you, inspector?'

'I am trying to find the next-of-kin of a man who was murdered on my patch. Our enquiries have led us to an address in Liverpool, The Elms, Wallasey Road. I understand that his father is a doctor, and that his name is Schumaker. Can I advise . . .'

'Schumaker, Doctor Haydn Schumaker?' Callahan said promptly.

Angel's face brightened.

'That's the one.'

'Bad news for you there, I'm afraid, wack. He was found murdered ten days ago now. On Christmas Eve.'

Angel's mouth dropped open. A cold shudder ran down his back.

Gawber noticed that something was wrong.

'I am on that case myself,' Callahan continued. 'It ruined my Christmas, I can tell you.'

Angel licked his lips.

'What happened?' he asked.

'He was found on Christmas Day morning. Gun shot. A .32, right between the eyes. He was one of these cosmetic surgeons, you know. Worked on society beauties, models and the like. Well somebody'd been working on him. Poor sod. When we found him, he was strapped to a bed and his mouth had been well and truly doctored with . . . something. He had lips like he'd been sucking a red hot poker!'

Six

Everywhere was sopping wet and the sky still gloomy as Angel turned the car into Barnsley Road. As it gained speed, he changed up to top and cruised along at a steady forty. The windscreen wipers were beginning to squeak on the glass now that it had stopped belting down. He reached out a finger to the control lever and stopped the racket. They were almost at Frillies, so Angel reached into his inside pocket, took out a dog-eared envelope and passed it to Gawber in the seat beside him.

'The address is on the back of there,' he said.

The sergeant took the envelope and looked at it bewildered as he scoured the small messy handwriting to find a sequence in the mass of words that looked like an address.

'According to Tickell, it was only a short distance from Frillies,' Angel said.

'The Brambles, Harrogate Road,

Clarendon,' Gawber suddenly began to read out. 'Is that it, sir?'

'Yes. He said it was near the country club gates. Almost opposite. Now that would be nice and handy for Schumaker to take a young lady out, wouldn't it?'

The painted gates of Frillies Country Club appeared on the right, and, almost immediately, on the left he saw a street sign that read Harrogate Road.

He tapped the indicator stalk, slowed and turned left down the narrow street with its modern architect-designed, detached and semi-detached houses set in pleasant-looking gardens liberally peppered with coniferous and deciduous trees. They looked attentively for a house sign and spotted it near the far end of the road. 'The Brambles', neatly painted in black on heavy, varnished, wooden, double gates.

Angel's eyes scanned the building for any alarm boxes or CCTV cameras. He couldn't see anything of that kind, but in the garden was an estate agent's board.

It said: 'For Sale. Penberthy's for Property. Telephone Bromersley 223942.'

He rubbed his chin. He turned to Gawber and said, 'Write that down, Ron. Surprising. The dead man's house is for sale already.'

They parked the car, walked through the gates and up the drive together past the small but well-kept lawn and borders. Gawber went straight on round to the back of the house, while Angel peeled off and made for the front door. He stood under the porch and looked round at the houses opposite and the neighbours either side. He needed to give Gawber a little time to get in position. He observed that he could be seen clearly only from the windows of the three houses opposite. He turned back, reached up for the knocker, gave the door four mighty thumps on the door, and waited. There was no reply, so he tried the handle. It was locked. He pushed hard against it. It was a substantial door; it didn't even shake. He went round the back and joined Gawber who was standing and waiting with his hands in his pockets.

'No signs of life, sir,' he said quietly, and pointed at the French windows. 'That lock looks the easiest bet.'

Angel looked closely at the keyhole, sniffed, then pulled a box of skeleton keys out of his pocket, chalked up a blank, inserted it in the keyhole and began the tedious process of picking the lock.

Meanwhile Gawber looked round to see if they could be observed by anybody. The large back garden comprised of thirty-six young apple trees planted in an area of adequately maintained turf, and, beyond that, a field of light brown, south Devon cows moaning loudly in their soaked surroundings. By the back door was a black rubbish bin on wheels. He lifted the lid expectantly and discovered it was empty. It was a disappointment. There were usually some useful treasures in and among the rubbish.

There was a click and Angel withdrew the two picks.

They were in.

Angel pushed open the glass door and Gawber followed.

The house was pleasant, airy, and spotlessly clean and tidy throughout, and was furnished with typical traditionalist furniture with a leaning towards minimalism in line with a bachelor's pad in the second millenium.

They made their way quickly through the sitting room, where there was a chest of drawers that Angel pointed to; then the kitchen, where there were more drawers and several cupboards, also an envelope projecting from behind a clock on the mantelpiece; there was a small pantry leading out of the kitchen; a dining-room with a sideboard with drawers and cupboards in it, a case clock in the hall that might conceal something. Angel also spotted a telephone and a message recording machine with a red light glowing. He stopped, went over to it and pressed the button. There was a hissing sound and then a woman's voice said, 'This is Doctor Bell's receptionist at the hospital. You've missed your appointment again, Mr Schumaker. Will you please phone to make another appointment? Thank you.'

Angel frowned. He looked at Gawber. They didn't speak.

They made their way up the stairs. There was a strong smell of something difficult to define but not unpleasant, like soap or flowers or perfume. The bathroom was bright and airy, assisted by the full-length mirrors all along one wall that looked like a recent DIY improvement. The bedroom had a large fitted wardrobe along one wall. Angel opened the doors and found that it was overflowing with men's clothes, smart suits, raincoats, overcoats, crisply pressed shirts on coathangers. Next to that was a separate cabinet holding a dozen or so smart pairs of leather shoes. There was a very comfortable double bed with a draped head and lots of pillows, bedside tables, lamps, and a dressing-table. The other room was a sort of study, a desk with lots of drawers, a swivel chair, built-in shelves filled mostly with reference books, maps, dictionaries, English and foreign.

Angel then said, 'Is there a loft?'

It was above the landing: a modern design with its own ladder. Angel found the pole and pulled down the ladder.

'This shouldn't take us too long, Ron. I'll look up here and do this floor.'

'Right, sir,' Gawber said, and made his way back down the stairs.

Two hours later, having searched every drawer and every cupboard and all the usual hiding places, Angel came downstairs with a cheque book and a folder of bank statements.

'That smell up there, can't think what it is.'

'Flowers, sir? A pomander? Or perfume of some sort? Smells expensive.'

Angel rubbed his chin.

'Thing is, I can't put it in a bottle and take it back to the lab,' he said, shaking his head.

He concluded that the rich smell was probably a French perfume. Schumaker had probably sprinkled it liberally on the bed linen, the towels, perhaps even the carpets. Angel rubbed his chin, but he hadn't spotted a spray or a bottle or any sort of a container.

Gawber had the envelope that had been behind the clock in his hand. He handed it to him. 'Letter from his dad. Probably contained a cheque.'

Angel grunted as he read it.

'It refers to a cheque that would have accompanied it, sir. It was from that address in Liverpool and dated two weeks back. It was probably intended as a Christmas present.'

He nodded.

'I've got his cheque book and bank statement for the Bromersley branch of the Northern City Bank. Did you find an address book?'

'No sir.'

'Mobile phone?'

'No. And the lad's very tidy and methodical.'

'Yes. Not a scrap of paper or an unnecessary hair in the place. And clean. Not a speck of dust. Very nice house, though.'

Gawber smiled.

'Spotless. I wouldn't mind living here, sir.'

Angel didn't hear him. He was thinking.

'I thought he would have had a mobile phone.'

'He would have had that on him, wouldn't he, sir?'

'You would have thought so.'

Angel looked round the kitchen.

'Is the place lived in, do you reckon? It's so hard to believe.'

'I think so,' Gawber said thoughtfully. 'I think it's his way. That's all.'

Angel wasn't sure.

He spotted the refrigerator and opened the door. It was well packed. He could see packets of bacon, sundry small items wrapped in white plastic paper with supermarket labels on them, plastic see-through boxes of strawberries and raspberries and so on. The door itself was loaded with margarine, cheese, cans of lager and plastic bottles of milk. He reached in and took one of the bottles out and looked at the label. 'Hmmm. Use by January 10th.' He looked at Gawber. 'Well, that's all right. Practically fresh. He must have bought that no more than a couple of days ago.'

'Yes,' Gawber agreed.

Angel squeezed the lobe of his ear between his finger and thumb.

'Have we finished then?'

'There's just the garage, sir.'

They went out.

Angel took the key out of the lock on the

109

inside of the French windows, shoved it in the keyhole on the outside, locked it and pocketed the key.

The garage was a simple brick-built, slate roof building. It was unlocked and inside was as immaculate as the house. The car in there was an expensive red Italian sports job.

When Gawber saw it, his mouth dropped open. He looked at Angel and then back at the car.

'There's about a hundred thousand quid there, sir. Good for pulling the girls, don't you think?'

Angel rubbed his chin.

Gawber smiled knowingly.

It was five o'clock, blacker than an under-taker's cat and freezing cold.

Angel parked his car on the service road behind Beckett's flats and made his way across the yard to the back entrance; he tapped in the code, then pushed open the security door, bounced up the steps, and dashed along the landing to flat number 12. He put the key in the lock, turned it and went inside. He was just in time to see the bedroom door close and hear the click of the latch.

He pursed his lips and went slowly up to it.

'It's only me. Michael Angel,' he called.

'Yeah. I'm coming,' Grady replied through the closed door.

Angel nodded, turned and looked round. The table was untidily littered with dirty crockery, cutlery and open packets and boxes of food, the remnants of a meal or two. There were more dirty pots on the draining board. He rubbed his chin. Grady had certainly made himself comfortable. He glanced down at the wastebin by the sink and saw an empty bottle with gold foil wrapping round its neck. He leaned down and snatched it up. His pulse quickened as he glanced at the label: Lafayette Champagne 1999.

His jaw tightened, he shook his head and dropped it back in the bin. It rattled noisily. His eyes wondered across to the bottom of the aluminium sink. There were more dirty plates and cutlery; it didn't look as if Grady'd washed up at all since his arrival, and then Angel saw two glass tumblers next to each other one of them marked at the rim with scarlet lipstick.

His pulse raced. The skin on the back of his hands tightened. He dashed over to the bedroom door, squeezed the doorknob and pushed at it hard. The door opened. It caught Grady on his backside. He was dressed in an open-necked shirt, slacks and slippers and leaning over the bed doing something with the pillows. He looked up. Their heads met six inches apart. Grady grinned slightly. Angel glared angrily into the man's big baby blue eyes. The policeman was so furious he could have bitten his nose off.

At the other side of the room near the window, he saw a slim young woman with a head of jumbled hair that covered her face. She was wearing a white blouse and a long leather skirt that she was vigorously yanking round her waist with both hands.

Angel's jaw dropped as he stared at her.

She glanced across at him momentarily, then turned away, unconcerned, and continued tugging at the skirt.

Grady straightened up and looked at Angel through lowered eyes; he was still smiling and rubbing his neck.

Angel's face was stonier than the Sphinx. He said nothing. He turned, stormed back into the sitting-room, thrust his hands hard into his coat pockets, blew out a long sigh and looked through the window at the sleet in the headlights of passing traffic.

Grady followed him out and closed the

bedroom door.

Angel turned round to him. He was the first to speak.

'Who's that, then?' he growled and jerked his head in the direction of the bedroom.

Grady rubbed his chin, then smirked and said, 'Sharon Rossi.'

Angel blinked and stared at him.

'*Sharon Rossi!*' he bawled.

Grady nodded. 'And I am going to marry her,' he replied robustly.

Angel shook his head. 'You're going to *die* for her!' he retorted. 'Sharon Rossi? Don't you realize when Rikki Rossi finds out about this, you're as good as a dead man.'

Grady's face changed. The smirk had gone. He was suddenly very serious.

'No. When he goes down he'll not be able to touch me.'

'There's Carl, and his mother, and that's Rikki's daughter in there. What's she going to think when she sees it's your evidence that has put her father away?'

'She knows all about it. I've told her. She hates her father. It was him that came between us before.'

'You can't trust her, you fool. She's having you for a right idiot! Blood's thicker than water. When her father presses the right buttons, she'll drop you faster than

113

the Lib Dems dropped Charlie Kennedy. You'll be as good as dead.'

Grady licked his lips. His eyes darted from left to right and then back again.

'No. No. She's . . . it's not like that,' he stammered.

'And you've just made the safest "safe house" in the UK into a death-trap,' Angel said, waving his arms round the room.

'No. She's all right. It'll be all right. She loves me. We can . . . I can still stay here.'

'Bah!' Angel snarled and wrinkled up his nose. 'That's what she *says*. But what does she really *think*? How will she react when she hears a jury declare her father guilty and sees them stick the cuffs on him and march him off to Wakefield for twenty years? What is she going to think about you then?'

'We've talked it all out. She's got a level head on her. She's a smart girl. She understands. I know what I'm doing.'

'Oh yes. You know what you're doing. That's why you're an unemployed bum, hiding out here at public expense, while she's prancing about in expensive clobber picking you up and dropping you down whenever she feels like it.'

'It's not like that.'

'But it is! It is exactly like that. And what are you going to use for money? A girl like that is not going to be satisfied with half a lager and a bag of chips, you know. That leather skirt she's wearing alone, I bet, cost the best part of five hundred quid. The idea of that lass and you is plain daft. It's riddled with difficulties!'

'No. It's not,' he snapped. 'And money is no problem, no problem at all,' he said, straightening up and sticking out his chest. 'I know where there's more than a hundred thousand quid. I can pick it up anytime I like.' He snapped his fingers, flamboyantly, and added, 'Just like that!'

Angel's eyebrows shot up.

'Honest money, is it? Not money that the law could send you down for? We've probably got all the numbers from the bank on file just waiting for a mug like you to get caught passing it!'

Grady couldn't think of a reply. He put his hands in his pockets and shrugged.

'And do you intend to marry her and have kids — unless you have the snip it's as likely as not — and then have her bring them to visit you every month at Strangeways? That's if you are still alive, of course, that's if you're lucky. She might not want to visit you, to see you with your blue-white prison tan, smelling of disinfectant, and with a permanent sniff from bunged up sinuses as

115

a result of condensation. You are not right in your head. Do you not see that this is a golden opportunity for you. A crossroads in your life. There are a million girls out there. It doesn't have to be this one. Send her back home. We'll move you to another safe house, although where to, I don't know at the moment. And then, next week, give your evidence, get Rikki put away, find yourself a proper job, a nice girl, get married, and get out of the rackets. That's what you should be thinking about, not trying to get one over on Rikki by bedding his daughter! It's ridiculous. And dangerous. Besides, you're old enough to be her father.'

'I told you, it isn't like that, Angel. She loves me and I love her. And I'm not that old. There's only twelve years in us!'

'Bah! It's enough. I've heard all that stuff before. I tell you, Rikki Rossi will think twelve is a lot. And I don't expect he has you in mind for a son-in-law!'

The bedroom door suddenly opened and Sharon Rossi slipped in. She closed the door and stood with her back against it. Angel hadn't seen her before that day. She was strikingly beautiful. His mouth dropped open as he stared at the attractive, slim face, high cheek bones and the delicately formed nostrils, slim nose and arched neck, similar features to her mother, of course, and with the advantage of youth. He didn't speak. He couldn't speak. He was thinking, she must be the sort of feminine form he'd heard that artists yearn to reproduce in stone and on canvas. He gazed at her face and then slowly tracked downwards, past the crisp white blouse buttons, the small belt buckle down to her pretty nylon covered ankles and chic leather shoes.

She stared at Grady and then at Angel.

'I have heard every word you've been saying,' she began.

Angel couldn't take his eyes off her. He listened carefully to her husky voice that sounded like warm liquid chocolate.

'Those walls are made of cardboard,' she continued. 'And you are quite wrong about me, Mr Angel. I love my father, but I don't *like* him. I have told Pete that I am a hundred per cent behind him.'

Grady smiled like a lottery winner in a trance.

She moved over to him, grabbed his arm and his hand and held tightly on to them.

'And it is true; we are going to get married, just as soon as dad is safely behind bars. And we are getting properly married in a church somewhere, because I love him, and because I am expecting his baby.'

■ ■ ■ ■

'*What!*' Strawbridge bellowed.

His voice made Angel's ear-drum ring. He pulled the phone away from his ear and held it at arm's length.

Angel's wife, Mary, looked up from the magazine she was reading and stared at him.

'Sharon Rossi's up the duff?' the superintendent repeated.

'Yes, sir.'

'Are you sure?'

'That's what she said.'

'Is she still at the flat?'

'Looks like she's moved in,' Angel said meaningfully.

'Well they're not having their honeymoon on public money, if I can help it,' he sighed. Then he said, 'I don't like this. I don't like this one bit. We can't do with this complication so near the trial. We can't do with this girl on the scene. There's no telling which way Grady will jump now. A bit of pressure from her and he'll say and do anything she tells him to. You should have stopped this.'

Angel's eyes flashed.

'How could I?' he said indignantly. 'I wasn't to know there was still anything between them. I couldn't have anticipated he would have contacted her.'

'All right. All right,' Strawbridge snapped.

There was a pause. The superintendent was thinking. 'I don't suppose there's any chance of her leaving voluntarily, or being persuaded to.'

'Shouldn't think so. There's only one thing I can think of, sir.'

'What?'

'Well, we know he's got a gun. I don't suppose he has a licence for it. Arrest him for being in possession of a gun without a licence. Bring him in and shove him in a cell. That'll kill two birds with one stone.'

'But we could only hold him for a few hours.'

'It's a start, isn't it?'

Strawbridge sighed.

'Arrest him now, and all the goodwill I have built with him will sail straight down the river. All that time wasted.'

'I don't know, sir. He still seemed pretty vindictive towards Rikki Rossi. And Sharon seemed red hot at supporting him. He may *still* be willing to give evidence.'

'Against her father? I wouldn't put money on it.'

'Do you want me to issue a couple of uniformed and go out and arrest him now, sir?'

'No. There is too much at stake; there's only a few days to wait. Let's leave things as they are. I'll sleep on it and see you in the morning.'

'Right, sir.' Angel sniffed.

'Good night.'

SEVEN

The morning came and Angel had expected to be called into Strawbridge's office early, but he heard nothing so he assumed the superintendent was prepared to let things at Beckett's Flats continue as they were. He wasn't very happy about it, but it wasn't his case. He was only acting as liaison between Strawbridge and Grady. He had enough on his plate so he was content to dismiss Grady, Sharon Rossi and the Walther from his mind.

There was a knock at the door.

'Come in.'

It was Ahmed with a handful of envelopes.

'Oh, it's you.'

He put the post on the desk in front of him.

'Yes, sir. And there's been a man on the phone. Didn't want to speak to you. Wouldn't give his name. Didn't give a number. Just left a message.'

'Oh? What's he say?'

'Will you meet him in the usual place at the usual time today.'

Angel smiled. Then nodded.

'He said you'd know who it was, sir.'

Angel nodded.

'Right. Ta. Anything else?'

'No, sir.'

There was a knock on the open door. It was DS Crisp.

'Come in. Right, Ahmed. Thank you.'

The cadet went out.

Crisp came in and closed the door.

Angel pointed to the chair.

'Have you sorted it out then?'

'Yes and no, sir,' Crisp said, sitting down and opening a file he had brought.

Angel wrinkled his nose.

'What do you mean?' he growled. 'You talk as daft as a politician.'

'Well, I went into the car showroom, sir, and managed to speak to the actual salesman. He said he had sold that car to a hard broad called Buller-Price.'

Angel frowned. 'How did she pay?'

'Cash, sir. Twenties and fifties.'

'Cash? All that, *in cash!* Didn't he think it was fishy?'

Crisp shrugged. 'Didn't say. Probably not. He was glad to make the sale.'

Angel pondered a moment.

'Did you get a description of the woman?'

'Yes, sir,' Crisp said and referred to his notebook. 'He said she was slim, red hair and had a mouth like a sink plunger.'

Angel blinked. Distinctive, he thought.

'Smart clothes. Wore a lot of gold jewellery. She came with a man. Could have been her chauffeur, he didn't get out of the car. She did all the talking and the paying.'

'How old was this bloke at the garage?'

'In his twenties, sir.'

Angel nodded knowingly. 'Anybody over forty would seem positively ancient to him. What about the insurance office?'

'Same woman. Paid cash, sir.'

'Mmm. Well, it all sounds very peculiar. Somebody trying to pretend that their name was Mrs Buller-Price? Hmmm. But I can't see why,' he said drumming his fingers on the desk.

'No, sir,' Crisp said. 'And I can't see that there's anywhere else to go. Her signatures will have to have been forged, but if we don't know who forged them . . .'

'Yes, quite. Mrs Buller-Price has done nothing illegal, and the car's not stolen. She's got herself a very nice motor, so that's OK.'

Crisp smiled.

'Very nice,' Angel said, while rubbing his chin.

His thoughts suddenly seemed to be anywhere but there for a few brief moments. Then his eyes lighted back on Crisp still in the chair by his desk, which brought him back to unyielding realism.

'Right,' he said in a businesslike manner. 'Get back to the country club to this murder. Liaise with Gawber. He's still looking for blood-stained, discarded clothes. The murderer would have wanted to have disposed of them quickly, burning fires, freshly turned earth, you know what to look for. And keep in touch.'

'Right, sir.'

Crisp went out and closed the door as Angel reached out for the phone.

'Cadet Ahaz,' came the smart, prompt reply through the earpiece.

'Ahmed. Get me Mrs Buller-Price on the phone.'

'Right, sir.'

A minute later, Angel heard her well-spoken, warm voice down the line.

'Hello, yes.'

'It's Inspector Angel here, Mrs Buller-Price. About your car. I'd like our traffic manager to take a look at it as soon as possible, make sure it is safe and roadworthy, you know. Take about an hour. How about this afternoon?'

'Of course, Inspector.'

'Bring it round the back of the station. Ask for Sergeant Malin.'

'Certainly will, Inspector. And thank you. You know it's time you came round for tea again. Haven't had a quiet talk with you for ages.'

Angel smiled.

'I have always said your Battenberg is the best I have ever tasted, Mrs Buller-Price, but time is the enemy of us all, I'm afraid.'

'I always have tea and cakes at four o'clock. I am usually on my own. Michael Caine and his beautiful wife called in yesterday on their way through to visit the new Archbishop of York. He remarked upon the lightness of my fairy cakes; he had four, and I gave him the rest to take with him. You would always be welcome. If I know to expect you, I'll make a point of having one of my special Battenbergs for you to try.'

Angel smiled. 'Thank you so much. That would be delightful. I hope to be able to call in very soon. Goodbye.'

He depressed the cradle to cancel the call, then dialled a number.

'Mallin. Traffic division.'

'Angel here. I have a little job for you,

Norman. This afternoon, Mrs Buller-Price is bringing a brand new car round for you to have a look at. I want you to see if it's roadworthy and safe for her to be tooting it round the place, in addition . . .'

Gawber looked up from the file he was reading and said, 'SOCO found the lager can under the settee, checked it for prints and there weren't any.'

Angel sniffed.

'That's odd. Very odd. He wasn't wearing gloves. Eloise, the girlfriend, the witness, said he wasn't wearing gloves. The beer can was thrown into the room. The girl said tossed in. Then the murderer came in immediately after it. How could it have been wiped clean?'

'Handkerchief, sir. Wiped it, before he threw it.'

'Yes. Would need a disciplined mind to do that: he would have to remember before he threw it, and hold it appropriately.'

'And, by the way, sir, it was a *lager* can,' Gawber said.

'Yes, of course. Is there any difference?' he growled.

'Not for throwing, sir. There would be for drinking.'

'Aye. Sounds as if it was deliberately

thrown to break up any atmosphere, possibly romantic atmosphere, that might have been created. After all, they were courting, had just had a nice meal, according to the girl. The room was quiet, pleasant, they were on their own on a settee.'

Gawber nodded.

Angel rubbed his hand across his chin.

'The entire scene is grotesque. The murderer wears a black mask, has a skull and crossbones tattooed on his hand, throws a lager can in just before he bounces into the room, and then enters waving a knife in the air, like a cutlass.'

He blew out a long sigh then shook his head.

'Do you know,' he continued. 'I believe this murder was executed as if it was part of a performance.'

'Like from a play, sir?'

'Could be. But no. No. Not exactly.'

'You mean a ritual?'

'No. I mean that he wanted to be seen committing the murder. He didn't commit the murder furtively, in the dark, up a back alley, alone. No. But in broad daylight, in a public place, in front of a witness. He even tossed in a lager can to herald his arrival.'

'But he wore a mask, sir.'

'Yes. That's odd too. It seems as if he

wanted to be seen, or be conspicuous, but not identified.'

'The witness said, she heard her boyfriend ask the man, "Why the mask?" '

'Yes. But he didn't reply. What do you make of that?'

Gawber shook his head.

'Don't make anything of it, sir. Do you?'

Angel looked down and shook his head. 'No.'

The church clock struck five.

Angel was at his desk with his nose in a heavy, wordy, inch-thick book: *The Home Office Review on ASBOs*. He was pleased that the church clock had rescued him from it.

He sighed; it was the end of an imperfect day. He was ready for home. He stuffed the book in his pocket, put on his coat and ambled up the corridor. He waved a hand at the constable at the reception window and pushed the door out into the cheerless cold winter evening.

The station steps were brightly lit, but as he reached the bottom and crossed the road, the only illumination was a cold, hazy moon. He walked on a hundred yards to Church Street, then took the corner down the side of the old wall to the heavy iron church gate. It opened with a slight squeal and clanged as he closed it. He walked, through tall Victorian gravestones, where the tops were visible in silhouette in cold moonlight along the flagstone path towards the porch door. Suddenly he became aware of lightweight, quick footsteps becoming louder. Someone was following him. It was a man who had the speed and dexterity of a dancer.

Angel slipped quickly on to the grass, hid behind one of the gravestones and waited. He could see the outline of a small man in a long, dark coat and smart hat perched at a jaunty angle. In profile, he could make out a very long nose shaped like a soup ladle. The man advanced rapidly and when he was a few feet away from him, he stopped, turned and rapidly looked around. Angel could hear his breathing. He could have reached out and touched him, he was that close.

Suddenly, the man turned to look in Angel's direction.

'Ah!' he said, in a crisp, cultured voice. 'You should never stand up wind of me, whoever you are. My senses are so finely tuned, I know that someone is there. I can feel the heat of your body.'

'Mr Helpman,' Angel said, stepping towards him. 'I am sure; I recognize the voice. I got your message. I hope it is worth my while.'

'Ah yes, Mr Angel. I have some information for you that is so hot you won't believe it. It's worth more than a hundred pounds to you, maybe several thousand, who can tell? But I will take only a hundred pounds for it, from you.'

Angel pulled a face, but in the dark there was no one to see it.

'You know, I haven't access to funds of that sort.'

'This is information you would sell your mother for, Mr Angel. And I offer it to you exclusively.'

He had had this conversation many times before with this man. So far as Helpman was concerned it seemed to be a necessary ritual. Angel's top money was always fifty pounds: all these negotiations were a waste of time. Both of them already knew how much money he was going to pay.

'You know that fifty quid is top whack, Mr Helpman.'

'This information could mean promotion for you, Mr Angel, superintendent at least, then chief constable.'

'Come along. It's fifty pounds or we can't do a deal. And it had better be worth it.'

'Mmm. Oh it's worth it. It's worth a great deal more. Make it a hundred.'

'I'm sorry.'

'I'll give you a hint. Whet your appetite.'

'I'll have to go,' Angel said and turned. 'It's been a long day.'

Helpman reached out and caught him by the coat sleeve.

'All right. All right,' he said quickly. 'Fifty it is. Let me have it.'

'If it's worth it, and after you have delivered,' Angel said patiently.

'Very well. You're very hard, Mr Angel. Very hard. So unyielding.'

'Come on. What is it? I've a hot meal and a warm fire beckoning me.'

'Yes. Yes. Yes, well. It's like this. You've got a new man in your nick, a tough, shrewd, hard man made up to a super by the name of Strawbridge, haven't you?'

Angel didn't reply. He was there to buy information not give any away free.

Helpman went on.

'It's common knowledge that Strawbridge got Rikki Rossi on remand on a charge of murder.'

'Go on,' Angel said encouragingly.

'Well, Rossi is on remand in Strangeways. In the next but one cell is a friend of a friend of an acquaintance of mine.'

131

Angel sighed.

'Sounds like a very distant relationship. Whatever it is, I hope it's reliable.'

'Oh it's reliable all right,' he said emphatically. 'Well, there were big celebrations last night on level one in 'B' block; that's the one Rossi's in. Rikki Rossi had just heard that his father, Stefan, who is doing twelve years in Wakefield —'

'I know that,' Angel said impatiently.

'Yes, well, he'd just heard that Stefan has done a deal with Stuart Mace, the man with the casinos and the girlie rackets, that will ensure that Rikki will go free.'

Angel's eyebrows shot up. '*Ensure* that he'll go free?'

'That's what was said.'

He licked his lips. 'How can he possibly do that?'

'Huh! I don't know that, Mr Angel. If I knew that, my price would certainly have been a thousand pounds. But you can rely on it. Rossi's brief, Solly Solomon flew up from London and they were chewing the fat for ages.'

Angel shook his head.

'Really?' he said, with a sniff.

'It will be so, Mr Angel,' Helpman said.

'How can you be so certain?' he said sceptically.

'I'll tell you how I can be so certain. A different source told me this. And I'll give this bit for free. There's a bookie in the prison, a chap called Otis. This morning, he opened a book on Rossi, and he's giving eleven to ten on, that the jury at the end of Rossi's trial will say not guilty. My friend says that Otis is never wrong.'

Angel knocked on the door.

'Come in,' the superintendent called.

He opened the door and put his head through the gap.

'I have some news, sir. You'll want to hear this,' he said significantly.

'Well, come in. Sit down.'

He took the chair by the desk.

'Thank you. Last night, a snout told me that he'd heard that Stefan Rossi had done a deal with Stuart Mace that will ensure that, at his trial next week, his son, Rikki, will be found not guilty, and will walk free. And that his barrister, Solly Solomon, who —'

Strawbridge's jaw dropped open. He was clearly taken aback.

'Rubbish!'

Angel looked at him and didn't reply.

'Who is this informer?'

'Reliable. Known him years.'

'How did he come by this information?'

Angel told him all that Helpman had said and concluded by saying, 'It may turn out to be incorrect, of course, but I stress, he has always proved to be spot on in the past. I shouldn't underestimate what this man says, sir.'

Strawbridge rubbed his chin. His hand was trembling.

'I need to see him,' he said urgently. 'I must milk him for every word, every nuance of what he claims, he knows.'

'You can't do that, sir.'

'Why not,' Strawbridge growled.

'Don't know where he lives.'

'You can tell me.'

'I don't know, sir. He blows in from time to time. Leaves a message for me.'

'Oh. Have you checked it for prints?'

'A verbal message, sir. On the phone.'

'We could trace the call.'

Angel shook his head. 'It'll be the public one at The Feathers. It always is.'

'Have they got CCTV?'

'Yes, but not in the phone box, but I know what he looks like. He's not on any wanted lists. He's a professional snout.'

'Is Helpman his real name?'

'Shouldn't think so.'

Strawbridge's eyes narrowed. 'You pay

134

money out for information to a man whose name you don't even know?' he bawled.

'In twelve years he's never sold me a turkey.'

'He will,' he said heavily.

Strawbridge rubbed his chin. The colour had drained from his cheeks. Suddenly he said, 'Right. There's no alternative. Draw arms and take two uniformed men and arrest Grady. But don't bring that girl, Sharon, in, for god's sake. Tell her to go back to her family. I expect her mother will be worried sick about her.'

Angel ran his tongue along his bottom lip.

'I wouldn't be sure about that, sir.'

Twenty-two minutes later, Angel was quietly navigating his car through parked vehicles on the service road at the rear of Beckett's Flats. He was closely followed by an unmarked police Range Rover. Inside the 4 × 4 were two uniformed sergeants in black-covered body armour and protective blue helmets; they were brandishing the very latest lightweight G36C Heckler and Koch rifles each fully loaded with thirty rounds. They stopped and parked on double yellow lines. The trio dashed quietly through the back gate across the yard. Angel tapped the code smartly into the back door lock and then they raced on tiptoe up the steps and along the corridor to flat 12.

Angel wanted to surprise Grady, avoid any sort of gun play and make a quick, quiet, orderly arrest. Possession of the Walther was the first priority. If Grady wasn't actually carrying the gun in his pocket or his waist band, Angel expected it to be under his pillow. He knew it was a dangerous operation, but he had the element of surprise.

He indicated to the two sergeants to keep well out of sight of the doorway as he offered the key to the door. The door unexpectedly responded to the touch and opened slightly. It wasn't latched and it wasn't locked! It swung open thirty degrees or so. Everything was quiet. There was no sign of life. Angel licked his lips. He hadn't expected this. He peered through the chink between the door and the door jamb. He could see the table still cluttered with pots and food. He could see the sink; there were more dirty pots piled up, half a loaf of bread, some cut slices and a knife on the draining board. Next to it was an electric toaster plugged into a socket in the wall. He looked across to the other side of the room. The bedroom door was ajar, but he couldn't see into it. It was uncannily quiet. He pursed his lips. He could hear the beat of his pulse throbbing in his ears; it was getting louder and faster.

He took two steps into the room, waited, looked round and listened.

He called out.

'Grady! Grady! It's Angel.'

Silence.

'Sharon! It's Angel!'

There was still no reply.

He took another two paces to the bedroom door. He put his hand up to it and gave it a gentle push. The blankets and pillows were in an untidy jumble across the bed. There was the smell of soap and humanity, but no sign of life. He ran his tongue over his bottom lip. He could hear his pulse beating faster and louder. He looked quickly around. There were no nightclothes, underwear, street clothes or any personal effects. He darted into the bathroom and the loo. There was nothing there. He yanked open the wardrobe doors. Two lonely wire coat-hangers swung and rattled on a bare rail. He pulled out the dressing-table drawers. There were no clothes or personal possessions there or anywhere else in the flat.

The birds had flown and they weren't coming back!

Strawbridge's eyes nearly popped out of his head.

'*What!*' he bawled, and jumped up from behind his desk. His hands were shaking, his lips twitching. '*They've gone?*'

'Yes sir,' Angel said, surprised at the strength of his reaction.

The superintendent's lips tightened.

'You should have anticipated this!' he said furiously. 'You should have seen this coming. Where could he have gone; where have they gone?'

Angel glared back at him. He hated injustice, especially when he was at the receiving end of it.

'I don't know, sir. On Tuesday night you decided to take the risk and it didn't come off!'

Strawbridge pulled a face as mean as an ex-wife chasing a maintenance order.

'I was determined to get Rossi permanently behind bars. Grady's evidence as a witness was the only way.'

Angel's face went scarlet.

'You shouldn't have let him have his gun back! Maybe unarmed he might have felt less confident at running off!'

Strawbridge glared across the desk at him.

'It's that tart, Sharon Rossi,' he sneered.

Angel agreed that she'd turn any man's head.

'I'm going to Strangeways,' Strawbridge snapped, reaching for his coat. 'I'll have to see Rikki Rossi: get him to change his plea.'

Angel blinked. He had as much chance of succeeding at that as there was of Ray Charles finding Tony Blair's Weapons of Mass Destruction.

EIGHT

'Come in, Ron,' Angel said. 'Shut the door.'

Gawber was carrying a big crumpled envelope.

'We've about finished out there at Frillies, sir. There are no recent diggings that we can see, and we've been through the waste-bins. Nothing.'

Angel sighed. It was hard going. Nothing was coming easily. He rubbed his chin.

'And can I talk to you about Ahmed, sir?'

'Ahmed? Yes. What's the matter?'

'Ahmed will be eighteen next week. I'm doing a whip round. Not often we get anybody coming of age on us. It's usually weddings, and leavings. I thought we could give him money, start him on his way. Unless you'd any plans of your own for him, of course.'

Angel sniffed and smiled. 'Eighteen, eh? Young Ahmed. I might have. What's everybody giving?'

'Mostly a fiver, sir.'

'Here's a tenner.'

'Thank you, sir.'

'I might be thinking of something original I could be giving him,' he said, pursing his lips. 'Remind me, will you?'

'Right, sir.'

Gawber went out and closed the door.

Angel could hardly imagine Cadet Ahmed Ahaz being a fully-blown adult. He would have to consider what memento he might give him. He was trying to recall what he had been given when he was eighteen and couldn't recall that he got anything.

His thoughts were interrupted by a knock at the door. It opened immediately and a man peered into the room.

It was the pathologist.

Angel looked up and smiled.

'Come in, Mac. Nice to see you.'

A short, white-haired man in his fifties came in with a file and a large plastic see-through envelope with the word EVI-DENCE in red printed diagonally across it.

'I was passing, Michael, so I thought I'd bring you the PM report. It's all finished.' He had a Glaswegian accent you could cut with a knife and spread on a bridie. 'And I've also brought the contents of the victim's pockets from SOCO.'

'Glad you did. Sit down.'

Doctor Mac placed the file and the envelope on the desk and took the chair nearest the desk.

'It's all finished,' Mac said. 'Did you discover the man's ID?'

Angel looked at him, smiled, lifted the file cover tentatively and then closed it.

'Oh yes. His name is . . . was Richard Schumaker. We've got his address. Don't know much about him. Appears to be single. His father was a plastic surgeon in Liverpool. He was also murdered recently.'

Doctor Mac shook his head compassionately and let out a short sigh. 'Oh.'

'What's the meat of it then?' Angel said. 'Save me wading through the Latin.'

'Very straightforward,' the shrewd Scot said. 'It's unquestionably murder. Young man, in his twenties, five feet ten inches, about a hundred and forty pounds, recent appendectomy scar. Died from heavy blood loss following an incisive wound with a pointed bladed instrument to the aorta. Would have died in less than twenty seconds. I have timed out the murder; it must have been between noon and 6 p.m. on Monday, the second.'

Angel sniffed. He'd heard it all a thousand times before, but post-mortems always

142

made him feel sad. He noted with a small amount of satisfaction that the time of death fitted Eloise Macdonald's account.

'What about the weapon, Mac, a pointed bladed instrument means a knife? What sort of a knife?'

The doctor shrugged.

'An ordinary domestic kitchen knife could have been used. Something with a blade up to half an inch wide. That's most any serious implement with a blade. There was nothing unusual or special at the aperture of the wound to assist with identifying the kind of weapon it might have been. Sorry about that. Something with a point at the tip and is a blade as opposed to a screwdriver or a meat skewer is what you'd be looking for.'

'Serrated?'

'Unsure. In this case, can't be certain. The knife was thrust in and then pulled out shortly afterwards, I think. The damage to the skin and the flesh was minimal and clean, and there was only the one incision straight into the artery.'

'Did you think the murderer was a surgeon or a butcher then?'

'Impossible to say, Michael. It could have been a lucky stab . . . I mean for the murderer of course.'

'Of course. Of course. Any other marks to the body? Needle marks, tattoos, you know what makes my tail wag.'

'No. Sorry, nothing there, Michael. And there was nothing under his fingernails of interest, just the usual dust in the air. The state of his lungs showed that he didn't smoke and that he was probably from round these parts. His stomach showed he had taken a meal just before he died. Nothing untoward in it. No poisons, nothing like that. His blood had an alcohol content. Quite a low level. It's all in there,' he said pointing at the file. 'It wasn't excessive. No drugs.'

Angel pursed his lips.

'Unusual. I thought everybody took drugs, except me . . . and you, possibly.'

Mac smiled.

'Any indications as to his likely employment, lifestyle?'

'Judging by his hands, he wasn't a manual worker. Soft and fleshy. His general muscle tone was quite good, and even. He might work out or jog or swim. Used a sunlamp, probably went to one of these local shops that have mushroomed.'

Angel's eyebrows lifted.

'How do you know he hasn't been in the hot sun in Barbados?'

144

'The line of his pants was too sharply defined.'

'Mmm. Anything else?'

'Aye. He had had a reasonable haircut quite recently. By that, I mean none of your short back and sides and a slop of Gloy by an opportunist tradesman. It was probably cut by a person who knew a bit about hairdressing.'

'Now how would you know that?'

'Simple. His neck had been shaved, which showed he had been attended to recently and the rest of his hair was tapered, as it should be, and not crudely shorn like a sheep from the outback. Also, it smelled of something pleasant, probably shampoo, or maybe brilliantine.'

'Mmm. Did his clothes tell you anything?'

'Middle of the road. Plain, good quality traditional dark suit, shirt and tie. Black leather shoes, wool socks. He was well turned out, conservative conventional, maybe a bit too traditional for the second millennium, but appropriate for taking a young lady he was wooing out to lunch.'

'Mmm.'

Angel rubbed his chin. He wasn't pleased. The evidence garnered so far wasn't going to solve the crime. The victim was a clean, decent young man, honesty oozing out of his every pore. His job would have been far easier if the victim had been up to his gills in Class A, was an alcoholic, a crook, a thief, a rogue and a vagabond.

He rubbed an ear lobe between finger and thumb.

'Thanks, Mac.'

The doctor took his leave.

As soon as the door closed, Angel reached out for the EVIDENCE envelope. He opened the flap and poured the contents on to the desk top. There was a handkerchief, bunch of keys, some coins, a silver clip holding two hundred pounds in notes, and a small crumpled unsealed brown envelope.

Angel opened the envelope and took out a piece of paper that might have been torn from an exercise book. It was folded twice. He unfolded it and was surprised to see that it was a handwritten list of names: about twenty girls' names, just the forenames, no surnames. The last entry at the bottom of the column was 'Eloise'.

He found a see-through file from a desk drawer, put the list in it and sealed the file down with sticky tape and put it on the desk in front of him.

Then he reached out for the phone and dialled a number.

A man's voice answered.

'Taylor, SOCO.'

'Yes. Angel. I'm looking at the contents of Schumaker's pockets. There's a sheet of paper document in there, a paper in an envelope, a list of names.'

'Yes, sir.'

'Were there any fingerprints on it?'

'Yes, sir. Pretty near a full set of Schumaker's and a smudged finger and thumb of another person's. Looked like a man's.'

'Aye,' Angel said thoughtfully. 'Thank you.'

'The file with all our findings will be coming through. Later today probably.'

'Hmm. Anything unusual?'

'Don't think so.'

Angel sniffed. 'Right.'

He replaced the phone slowly, rubbed his chin and wondered if he was in a tunnel that didn't have a light at the end of it.

St Peter's church clock chimed the half-hour.

Angel could often hear it in his office when it was quiet and the wind was blowing from the east, which was also the certain indication in January of lower temperatures. He looked up from the letter he was reading, pulled back his sleeve and looked at his watch. Yes, it really was half past five. He

147

sniffed. It was not the end of a perfect day. He signed the letter and closed the folder. He put the top on his pen and dropped it into his pocket. He squared up the pile of papers, folders and envelopes in front of him and slotted them into a desk drawer. He blew out a long sigh and rubbed his scratchy chin. If he had had to give an account to God about what he had achieved that day he would have had to admit that it wasn't very much. He stood up and reached out to the hook for his raincoat. He didn't intend being home late that night.

He glanced at the window. Outside was as black as a plumber's thumbnail. His window looked out on to the side of a large Georgian house long since converted into council offices. The wall was in darkness so it returned no images, and by night assumed the role of a mirror. He noticed a reflection of his ample shape and turned quickly away.

He closed the office door, walked briskly up the corridor, waved a hand to the constable on the counter and pushed through the glass door out of the station. He paused on the top step and looked out into the night. It was already cold. He reckoned there would be a hard frost later that night. He stabbed his hands into his pockets and skipped lightly down the stone steps to the pavement.

Unusually, he was going to call at the off-licence and pick up a bottle of red for Mary. He'd been home late every evening that week and had caught it in the neck from her each time as she had struggled to keep a hot dinner edible. She imbibed hardly at all, and not on a regular basis, so he hoped the vino would cheer her up.

He reached the main road, stopped, looked both ways and then picked his way across it, dodging between a slow-moving black car and a bus that had just stopped for passengers. He then turned down left along the side of the church wall, past the gates, round the corner again to a ginnel that provided a short cut through a row of old houses to a small parade of shops comprising a newsagent's, a tobacconist's, a confectioner's and Heneberry's off-licence. There were no pedestrians around; they had had the good sense to make for home in the daylight.

The main street was well illuminated. The rain of an hour ago on the pavements and road surfaces had provided a sheen that reflected light from the sickly-coloured halogen lamps.

He went under the arch into the ginnel. He could barely see the dim light of a lamppost at the other end that opened into a cobbled yard, where the rear entrances to the shops were located and deliveries made. He continued picking his way on the cobbles considering whether he should get a bottle of South African or one of the new Australian wines and trying desperately to blank out the annoying details of the mystery surrounding the murder of Richard Schumaker, when suddenly he heard a footstep behind. It was followed immediately by a blow to the back of his neck, that felt like one of Fred Dibnah's chimneys collapsing on him. He buckled to the ground. He instinctively put his hands out to limit the damage of hitting the cobbles. The pain on his neck was wicked and hot and raced up to his head. He quickly pushed himself up but received a further whack to his back as he was straightening up. He gasped. He went straight down and immediately tried to get up again. Under his arm he caught sight of the silhouette of a man wielding something long and shiny; he couldn't see quite what it was. He put his hands up to protect his head when another blow caught him across the ear and another on his arm. The blows stung more than a thousand wasps. Through the continued assault, he managed to get to his feet, and backed away keeping his hands in front of him. The attacker advanced relentlessly. Angel rolled against the wall trying to dodge the blows. He saw the weapon was a baseball bat. The blows kept coming. His arms took most of the damage. He was getting to know when to expect them and at what angle they would next come. He took the opportunity and reached out for the weapon. Then suddenly, he felt a blow from behind. He turned and saw another figure wielding a bat. The outline of the head was different. The figure was shorter. It looked like a woman! It was a woman! She was wearing something dark across the bottom half of her face.

The limited light from the lamppost caught her eyes: they shone like a tiger's. Blows now showered on him from every direction. He made a grab for the man's bat and eventually got a hold on it with one hand. He struggled to take it off him, while blows continued to rain mercilessly on him from behind. He maintained the grip on the bat now with both hands but slipped down on the cobbles. The man had to come down with him.

'Angel, you bloody swine!' the woman snarled, continuing to lam into him. 'Where is Pete Grady? Where is Pete Grady?'

He now knew his attackers were Carl and Gina Rossi, brother and mother of Rikki.

'I don't know,' Angel gasped. 'But if I did know, I wouldn't tell you.'

'You pig,' she spat at him.

He felt another blow to the head, followed by a kick on the shin from a pointed shoe, no doubt with a Gucci label.

'If Grady appears as a witness against Rikki next week,' Carl Rossi snarled. 'Your wife is going to be busy choosing a wooden box.'

'And it needn't be a big one,' Gina added. 'By the time we've finished with you, a pencil box will be too big!'

A two-note siren echoed in the distance.

'It's the police, Ma,' Rossi gasped.

'Come on,' she replied urgently.

Angel heard the uneven clatter of high heels on cobbles fade quickly away up the ginnel. He wiped the sweat from his eye and discovered it was red and sticky.

The car siren was now much louder. There was a screech of brakes followed by the slamming of car doors.

Angel was still holding the baseball bat handle. He got to his feet panting and leaning against the wall. There was silence. His mouth and jaw stiffened. His fingers tightened round the bat handle. He looked at it for a second then he threw it with tremendous force down the yard. It rattled noisily as it bounced on the cobblestones like a skeleton dancing on a xylophone. The effort caused him pain; he nursed the bruised arm across his middle. He had a foul taste in his mouth. It felt sore. He spat something out.

Heavy footsteps came running up behind him.

He turned towards them.

'Is that you, sir? Are you all right?'

It was Crisp.

'Of course I am,' he bawled angrily, wiping his mouth. 'You've scared them off, just as I was getting top side of 'em!'

Another constable arrived.

'There were two of them, sir!'

'I know that, you bloody fool! Well, don't just stand there like a couple of fairies! Get after them!'

'Right, sir.'

They turned to run back up the ginnel.

'And be careful!' he yelled.

'Come in,' Strawbridge bawled.

Angel pushed open the door.

The superintendent looked up at him.

'Come in. Sit down.'

Angel closed the door but said nothing.

Strawbridge stared at the cut on his

temple and the swollen purple patch under his left eye.

You're a mess,' he added with a sneer. 'You shouldn't be here.'

'I'm all right, sir,' he grunted.

'You were damned lucky Crisp and Scrivens turned up.'

Angel snorted.

'Huh! They scared them off! Just as I was getting on top of 'em!'

'You didn't say who tipped them off.'

'Somebody rang in. Told reception I was being followed down the ginnel. They happened to be passing in a car. That's all.'

'Who was the good Samaritan then?'

Angel knew that the only person it could have been was his snout, Helpman, but he wasn't saying.

'Didn't give his name.'

'Mmm.'

Angel needed to reverse the line of fire, put Strawbridge on the defensive.

'What did Rossi say then, sir,' he said, with his tongue in his cheek. 'Is he going to change his plea?'

Strawbridge frowned and the corners of his mouth turned down. He leaned forward and spoke urgently.

'That's what I want to see you about. *We have got to find Grady!*'

Angel just looked at him. He took it that the answer to his question was 'no'.

'If we don't find him by Monday, Rossi might walk free!' Strawbridge yelled.

Angel rubbed his chin.

'What I don't understand, is that Stefan Rossi is supposed to have done a deal with Stuart Mace that will stop Grady from giving evidence. My snout told me as much!'

'Well your snout's got it wrong. I said that before.'

Angel frowned then shook his head. Helpman had always been a hundred per cent reliable.

'We've got to find Grady. We must find Grady and bring him in.'

Angel shook his head. 'Where would we start?'

Strawbridge looked closely at him, ran his tongue over his lip a few times and then said, 'Are you sure it was Gina and Carl that assaulted you last night.'

'Positive,' Angel said. 'She spoke to me, threatened me. Told me if Grady appeared in court next week they'd kill me, put me in a box,' he added with a grim smile.

Strawbridge didn't smile.

'Must have been stalking you. Bit off their patch, isn't it? This side of the Pennines in winter, can be very dicey driving in the dark over Woodhead.'

'Where do the Rossis live?'

'We don't know. Nobody knows. They keep moving. It is thought that they have at least four places in Manchester, then a house or a flat or something in Florida. Gina boasts that they never sleep in the same pad two nights running.'

Angel nodded knowingly.

'It'll not be to show off how wealthy they are. It'll be because they have an obsessive desire to waken up every morning, still breathing!'

Strawbridge wasn't listening.

'I told you that girl would betray Grady. I blame her!'

Angel rubbed his chin as he thought about the beautiful Sharon.

Strawbridge suddenly slammed a hand on the desk and stood up. 'Where is he? Where the hell is he?' he said loudly and waved his arms in the air.

The phone rang.

Strawbridge snatched it up.

'Yes? . . . Who?' he said incredulously.

His jaw dropped. He stared across at Angel.

Angel knew it was something huge.

'Are you sure? . . . Right. Put him through.'

Strawbridge put a trembling hand over the

mouthpiece and whispered, 'It's *Grady!*'

Angel's mouth dropped open. He watched Strawbridge's twitching fingers squeeze and then slacken their grip round the handset four times before he said a word.

'Hello Peter, where are you? What did you run off for?' he began.

Angel cringed. He was talking to Grady like Angel's grandmother used to speak to him a hundred years ago.

'You can tell me,' Strawbridge continued. 'I'll come for you, or Michael Angel and I. You'll be perfectly safe in a convoy of armed police. You can bring Sharon and . . . Suit yourself. . . . Yes. Monday, ten o'clock. I'll be watching out for you. . . . Yes. Court number one.'

There was a loud click through the earpiece.

Angel heard it.

'He's gone.' Strawbridge sighed. 'Says he'll definitely be there on Monday.'

Angel nodded.

Strawbridge didn't look pleased. He put a hand on his chest and pulled a face as if he'd just swallowed a cucumber whole.

'Where is he now?' Angel said urgently. 'Where was he ringing from?'

Strawbridge shook his head, banged on the phone cradle and dialled a number. 'I am about to try and find out. I expect he was speaking from a mobile.'

His call was promptly answered.

'This is Detective Superintendent Strawbridge of Bromersley Police speaking. About a minute ago, on an extension of this landline, I was speaking to a man whose life is in very great danger. . . .'

Angel left the superintendent trying to trace the source of the phone call. He reached his office, closed the door and looked at the fresh pile of papers, files and envelopes that had arrived on his desk that morning and sighed.

Ahmed came into the office and brought him a cup of tea. The cadet noticed the purple swelling under the inspector's eye, but didn't say anything.

'Ta,' Angel said. 'A little job for you. Ring CRO and see if we have anything on this Richard Schumaker. And let me know pronto.'

'Right, sir.'

'And there's something else. There's an estate agent's, Penberthy's. Ring them up and ask them who instructed them to offer the house, The Brambles, out at Clarendon, for sale, and when. All right?'

'Right, sir.'

He went out as Crisp came in carrying a videotape. He glanced at Angel's face and did a double-take.

'Nasty, sir. Good job we came along when we did.'

'What!' Angel bawled. 'You let them get away!' he added irritably. 'Now what do you want?'

Crisp's mouth dropped open. He didn't respond. He held up the video.

'I couldn't see many hands, sir, to check whether they had a tattoo on them or not. Most of the members seemed to be well over forty. There was only one man who could be described as young, tall, and dark-haired and that was the waiter, Louis Dingle.'

Angel pursed his lips.

'I thought the chef, Walter Flagg would also have filled the bill.'

Crisp nodded.

'I met him, sir. Yes. But he hasn't a tattoo.'

'I know that,' Angel said impatiently.

'Ah, well, he probably used the back entrance to the kitchens being the chef, of course.'

'How many people came in and out, approximately, during that twenty-four hour period?'

'Between a hundred and a hundred and

twenty, I suppose.'

Angel rubbed his chin.

'Martin Tickell is only about thirty, sir. I haven't included him either.'

'Right,' he said thoughtfully.

Angel couldn't hide his disappointment. That videotape hadn't added anything to what he already knew. He reckoned it was time that the inquiries started being fruitful.

'Now. I know that Schumaker banked at the Northern City Bank. Nip down there, get copies of his bank statements for at least a year back, details of his standing orders, and you know what else.'

'Right, sir.'

Ahmed knocked on the door and pushed in without waiting.

'Excuse me, sir. The super wants the London phone book, P to T. And he says it's desperate. Have you got it in here?'

Angel swivelled round to the table behind him and scanned it.

'P to T? Whose number is he looking for? I might have it.'

'A barrister called Solomon, sir.'

Angel's eyebrows shot up. He swivelled back round.

'No. I haven't got it, and I don't know Solly's number.'

Ahmed frowned.

'Thank you, sir,' he said, and rushed out.

Crisp said, 'I'll get off to the bank.'

The door closed.

Angel rubbed his hand slowly across his mouth. If Strawbridge wanted Solly's number then something important must have happened. He couldn't think what. No doubt Strawbridge would tell him if it mattered. Must get on. . . .

He reached out for the phone and dialled a number.

A familiar voice answered: 'SOCO. DS Taylor.'

'Yes. It's Angel here. I want you to check out a house.'

'Right, sir. Can't do it today.'

'That's all right. I'll be away at Manchester Crown Court next Monday. Do it sometime then.'

'I can manage that all right, sir. What's the address?'

'Good. You know that lad that was murdered at the country club on Monday? It's his place. It's a very nice house; I think it's been quietly used as a secret love nest. Wouldn't be surprised if you find a certain young lady's prints all over the place.'

NINE

Angel drove his car up to the front of Bromersley police station and pulled on the handbrake. It was exactly eight o'clock on Monday morning, 9 January. It was gloomy and cold, but fine and dry. It was the day that the Lancashire and South Yorkshire police forces had long been waiting for: the opportunity to put Rikki Rossi behind bars for a good long stretch.

Angel looked up the station steps to see if the superintendent was there. He wasn't. He sniffed. He spotted a piece of fluff on his coat sleeve; he picked it off and disposed of it through the car window. He looked very smart, smarter than usual; Mary had insisted that he wore his new suit and the shirt she had ironed specially for him, and he looked as smart as a cabinet minister on the pull. He had given evidence at Manchester Assize several times before and so the day was not particularly highly charged for him. The outcome of course, was very important for law and order, the legal system and the national police force, but it was the superintendent's day and not his. He hadn't any exacting responsibility. He wasn't a witness, he was there merely to act as Strawbridge's chauffeur and to assist with any arm twisting that might be necessary to get Grady into the witness box and deliver his crucial evidence. Given choice, he would have much rather have stayed there in Bromersley and continued the investigation into the mystifying murder of Richard Schumaker.

He spotted movement out of his eye corner. It was Strawbridge; he was running down the station steps. He reached the pavement, opened the car door and jumped in.

'Good morning, sir.'

'Good morning, Michael.'

The door slammed shut.

Angel released the handbrake and let in the clutch.

They were soon on the Pennines. Provided the roads were clear and there was no snow at the top, the journey should take about an hour and a half. That would allow time to park the car, meet up with Grady and the CPS's legal team led by Oliver Twelvetrees and then get a seat in the court.

Strawbridge was in a thoughtful mood, and sat quiet as Angel pressed the car westwards up the Pennines past the reservoirs and through the forests of coniferous trees.

The superintendent suddenly sighed and said, 'Do you really think Grady will show up?'

Angel considered the question for a moment or two. It was almost impossible to answer. Grady might intend to appear and yet get cold feet at the last minute. But anyway, he thought it would be better to keep Strawbridge in an optimistic mood.

'Yes. I should think so. Why not? He hates Rossi. For him this will be payback time.'

Strawbridge nodded and rubbed his chin.

It was difficult to judge whether or not he was convinced.

Angel noticed a sign that said, 'Welcome to Lancashire.' He checked his watch. They were making good time. The sky was brightening and there was no sign of any snow.

'Would you put money on it, Michael?' Strawbridge suddenly said.

Angel shrugged.

'Yes,' he said, trying to sound convincing.

'Five hundred quid?' Strawbridge said tentatively.

Angel pursed his lips. He thought he sounded in earnest.

'I couldn't afford to lose that much, sir.'

The superintendent's face showed that he wasn't pleased.

'A hundred then? You don't sound that convinced. Put your money where your mouth is.'

Angel grudgingly said, 'A tenner. That's as far as I can go.'

'Right. You're on,' Strawbridge said eagerly. 'A tenner it is,' he said with a sniff. 'You're not overwhelming me with confidence, Michael.'

Angel said nothing. He saw a sign that said 'Manchester 12 miles'. He put his foot down harder on the accelerator.

Angel turned into Deansgate then Bridge Street scanning each side of the road for a place to park. The car-park on Gartside Street was full, which was a surprise. He made his way along Quay Street then Peter Street and eventually found a multi-storey near St Anne Street. This hunting for a place to park made them later than expected reaching the court building. They eventually arrived on the stone steps, breathless, and joined the short queue in the drizzle outside the main door. Eventually they were frisked by two friendly, but businesslike, uniformed sergeants from the Lancashire force and admitted into the noisy, crowded corridor that led to the courtrooms.

It was 9.55 a.m. exactly.

They pushed through the throng of men and women in gowns and wigs, men in morning suits and people in ordinary street clothes, who were gathered in groups, some talking, some listening and all looking deathly serious. Angel followed Strawbridge as he weaved his way through the people down to the CPS office where he knocked on the door.

A man in a robe and wig pulled it open and stood there staring at them. Beyond him, Angel could see four men similarly clad talking intimately in a huddle.

'I'm looking for Mr Twelvetrees,' Strawbridge said loudly.

The tallest man in the group heard his name. He broke away and approached the door.'

'Ah. Superintendent Strawbridge, isn't it?' he said crisply. 'I have no time to speak now. We have just been called.'

Strawbridge nodded.

'Where's Grady?' Twelvetrees asked. 'I have some points to go through with him.'

'Coming independently. I thought he

would have been here by now.'

'Haven't seen him.'

The three barristers came out of the room and pushed past them making their way into the corridor. The door closed.

'I have to go. When he arrives, bring him here. And tell my clerk.'

Twelvetrees dashed off, his black robe streaming behind. Two other men in morning suits carrying briefcases, who had been hovering nearby, joined him and they swept through the big doors together.

Strawbridge and Angel looked round.

Surprisingly, the corridor was now almost deserted. There were long wooden seats down the middle of the area and about fifty or so people, presumably witnesses and solicitors, remained. Some were drinking tea out of plastic cups. Two policemen carrying Heckler and Koch G36C rifles walked slowly by.

The big clock on the wall above the doors to the courts showed that it was exactly ten o'clock.

Strawbridge pointed to a vending machine.

'Get me a tea, Michael? I'll just have a word,' he said and wandered up the corridor to the main door.

Angel found some coins from his pocket,

fed the machine and pressed the buttons. Then he watched Strawbridge approach one of the sergeants on the door; he flashed his warrant card and began talking to him. Then he pulled something out of his inside pocket and showed it to him. It was a photograph. The sergeant looked at it, nodded and handed it back. He said something else, seemed pleasant enough and concluded by nodding his head. Strawbridge waved acknowledgement and came back down the corridor, but he didn't look pleased.

'He hasn't seen Grady,' he said. 'But he's heard of him. He recognized him from the photo. He says he'll keep an eye open for him and let me know when he arrives. This is the only way into court number one. So he has got to come through that door.'

Angel nodded and handed Strawbridge the plastic container of tea. He noticed that the superintendent's hand was shaking.

'Ta.'

Angel glanced surreptitiously at his sombre face. He was not a happy man. He must feel under considerable pressure.

They sat on the central aisle seat sipping tea.

The clock was ticking away. An usher came into the corridor occasionally and called out a name. People got up from the seats and went with him through the door to the courts.

There were a few new arrivals filtering through the main door.

Strawbridge looked across anxiously to see if any one of them was Pete Grady.

Time ticked away.

The clock showed 10.35 a.m.

Angel was beginning to think he had lost his tenner.

A blue vein on Strawbridge's temple began to throb.

Angel looked round for something to read; there wasn't anything.

A few more witnesses were admitted into the big corridor.

Then suddenly, a uniformed police constable carrying a rifle strode heavily in their general direction.

Angel wondered if he was coming to speak to them.

The man's face looked grim.

Strawbridge stood up expectantly.

'Are you Superintendent Strawbridge, sir?'

Angel knew something was wrong. Very wrong.

'Yes,' Strawbridge said. 'What is it?'

'You're waiting for a witness, a Peter Joseph Grady, aren't you?'

169

Strawbridge stared at him.

'Yes,' he said, hanging on his every word.

'Duty sergeant has asked me to pass on a signal, sir. Just come through on his radio. A body has been found under a pier at Blackpool. It has a bullet wound through the forehead. It's not been formally identified, but it is thought to be that of Peter Joseph Grady.'

Angel felt as if he had been belted in the stomach with a grave-digger's shovel.

Strawbridge simply lowered his head for a second, rubbed his hand across his mouth, then raised his head back up and gave out a long sigh.

'Come in, Ron.'

'Good morning, sir.'

'Is it?' Angel grunted.

Gawber closed the door. He was carrying a large envelope.

'I heard the news, sir.'

Angel leaned back in the swivel chair.

'Aye,' he growled and pointed to his bloodshot eye. 'To think, I got this all for nothing.'

'What happens now, sir?'

Angel grunted.

'The CPS will try to take the case as far as they can, or the judge might immediately

170

throw it out. The crown can't possibly win, and Rikki Rossi will be discharged without a stain on his character!'

'Nothing to be done?'

'Not unless the Lancs police can prove that Carl or Gina, or both, murdered Pete Grady. He was shot between the eyes; it is their trade mark. But the scene of crime had been washed by the Irish sea, twice, so I doubt they'll get much forensic.'

'They'll need a lot of luck.'

'And it's certain there'll be no witnesses!'

'It's not right.'

Angel's lips tightened.

'Tell me about it,' he growled.

He noticed the envelope.

'What you got there?'

Gawber opened it and pulled out a glossy photograph.

'That missing model, Tania Pulman,' he said. 'I was thinking, could we circulate it to the newspapers? She's a bit of a bobby dazzler. I reckon they'd be pleased to print it on their front pages. Maybe the TV people would also be willing to make an appeal?'

Angel looked at the colour photograph and nodded. He had to agree that she was indeed a beautiful young woman.

'How long has she been missing now?' he said handing back the photograph.

'Twenty days. Almost three weeks.'

'Got a written description?'

'Yes,' Gawber said. He turned the photograph over and read off the back, 'Five feet eight, blonde hair, blue eyes, twenty-two years of age, wearing a pink dress, brown leather coat, carrying matching designer Boucheron handbag with fastener formed from two intertwining gold snakes.'

Angel blinked.

'Gold snakes?'

'Gold-plated, I expect, sir. Although I was told the bag cost over five hundred pounds!'

'Five hundred pounds?' Angel boomed.

He shook his head.

'Overpriced designer rubbish. And how far have you got?'

'Nowhere, sir. Checked on her relations, ex-boyfriends, people at work, bank account, credit cards, mobile phone . . . nothing at all.'

'All right, give it a go, but you deal with it. I've got plenty on. And I don't want to get tangled with the TV people again. I had enough of them in that man in the pink suit case, last year. They drive you potty. And is that a fair photograph? It's no good using an airbrushed glamour pic if she really doesn't look anything like it. Nobody is going to recognize her.'

'I'll check it out with her parents.'

There was a knock at the door.

Angel pointed to it.

Gawber stood up and pulled it open.

It was Ahmed. He was carrying an envelope.

'Come in. Now what is it?'

'I've heard from CRO, sir. There's nothing on Richard Schumaker.'

'Hmmm. Thought there wouldn't be. Right. Ta.'

'And this letter was handed in for you, sir. I think it's from SOCO.'

He passed it across to Angel and turned to go.

'Hang on, Ahmed. I've got a little job for you.'

Angel tore into the envelope.

'Yes, sir?'

'Yes. I want you to make some enquiries. I am looking for a Dr Bell; see if you can rustle up a doctor or surgeon of that name, in a GP practice, a private practice, hospital, the NHS, BMA or whatever. It seems Richard Schumaker was seeing a doctor by that name. I don't know what for, or indeed anything else, just the name, Dr Bell. See what you can do.'

'Right, sir.'

Ahmed went out.

'Grand lad, that,' Gawber said. 'It's his birthday next week, eighteen.'

'Aye,' Angel grunted, his head in the letter. 'I hadn't forgotten.'

The envelope contained a letter from DS Taylor of SOCO; stapled to it was an A4 sheet listing locations on domestic furniture and fixtures.

Angel frowned, looked up at Gawber, passed him the letter and said, 'Read that.'

It said:

For the attention of DI Angel.

Dear Sir,

Further to your instructions, we have completed the search for fingerprints on the residential premises and home of the deceased, Richard Schumaker, known as The Brambles, Harrogate Road, Clarendon, Bromersley.

We found no prints of the deceased, but found your prints in forty-eight places and those of DS Gawber in thirty-seven places.

All prints found were identified, and the locations detailed on list attached.

The premises were secured and the key to the French window has been returned to Cdt Ahaz.

Yours sincerely,
D. Taylor (DS).

Gawber looked across at Angel.

'That's very odd, very odd.'

Angel nodded.

'That means that before we broke in and searched the place, Richard Schumaker or somebody else had already been round every nook and cranny with a duster, nay, I daresay a rag soaked in spirit, and carefully wiped every surface that would have accepted a fingerprint. Now what do you make of that, Ron?'

'Creepy, sir.'

The phone rang.

He reached out for it.

'Angel.'

'It's DS Taylor, sir.'

'Yes, Don?'

'You were right, sir. We've found the body of a partly clothed woman behind that wall of mirrors in the bathroom.'

Angel's heart began to pound. The hair on the back of his hand stood up. He blew out a long sigh. He had been sussing out dead bodies for over twenty years, but he still couldn't get used to it.

'Right,' he grunted.

'And the smell is now stronger than yesterday and different. It's the combination of perfume and putrefaction. Whoever put her there, doused her and her clothes with perfume.'

Angel nodded. That's where his thoughts had wandered to, but he didn't feel the slightest satisfaction in having his idea confirmed.

'Been there long?'

'The house is warm, central heating is on, we are talking two weeks or more, I should think, sir. Dr Mac has been notified; he's on his way.'

'Right, Don. I'll see you later. Goodbye.'

Angel replaced the phone, and thoughtfully rubbed his chin. This was a bad business, a very bad business indeed. It was true that close on Christmas, and just after, was the busiest time in the murder business. But this festive holiday had been a particularly bad time. He shook his head. Strange lad, that Schumaker. There must have been some very curious activities pursued in that house. He wished he knew what had been going on.

There was also a dearth of information about the lad's murderer. All Angel knew was that he was looking for a tall, young man, with dark hair, skull and crossbones tattoo on the back of his left hand; that some of his clothes would be sprayed with blood; that he stole a coat and gloves from the cloakroom; that he was a bit of an actor and that, that was about it.

If only the man's mobile phone could be found, Angel would then be able to find out who he had conversed with on a day-by-day basis. He could interview them; that might throw up a suspect. He might also learn what his interests had been, apart from women!

There was a knock at the door.

'Come in.'

It was DS Crisp.

'Got a copy of Schumaker's bank account, sir. Nothing strange or unusual. Just that he gets eight hundred pounds a month from a bank in Liverpool. Traced it back, it's from his father. A direct credit.'

Angel's eyebrows lifted.

'That's a generous daddy.'

He rubbed his chin.

'Are there any other sources of income?'

'No, sir. All he seems to pay out are ordinary utility bills: credit card, gas, electric, telephone, and so on.'

Angel's eyes narrowed.

'No mobile phone?'

'No, sir.'

'I wonder if he really had one?'

Angel drove on to the car-park of Cheapos, the supermarket, located on the edge of Bromersley. He parked near the store entrance and walked purposefully towards the main double doors of the massive one-storey glass and plastic building. He dodged a dozen shoppers with juddering trolleys rattling past him travelling in every direction, and glanced at the signs that extolled the virtues, the value, the low prices, and the special offers available from the store that claimed to be the biggest and cheapest in town.

He made himself known at the enquiry counter near the door and asked for Miss Eloise Macdonald. The staff were extremely courteous and helpful: it was no problem at all.

While he waited, he was offered the tasting of a new cheese, which he politely declined, was offered leaflets on banking, double-glazing, car and home and pet insurance and membership of a vehicle breakdown service. He accepted all the leaflets and pushed them into his pockets to save explanation and time.

A lady told him all about the voucher

system that rewarded customers who spent more than fifty pounds, with a free Cheapos Lucky Bag worth a pound.

He smiled. It must have been forty years since he remembered anything of a lucky bag, which he recalled he had bought in those days from a little shop on the corner for a small nominal coin and was always giant value. The lady carefully explained the worthiness of the Cheapos Lucky Bag and gave him a leaflet detailing the typical contents, the breakdown value and told how much children would enjoy their many and varied contents. He patiently took the leaflet. It was easier than explaining that he hadn't any children, didn't know any children and was unlikely to come across any children.

'You want to see me, Inspector?'

It was Eloise Macdonald looking very attractive in a blue overall.

She appeared behind the counter. She showed him into a tiny room close by. Angel looked round. It had a table and four chairs, and was probably where the store security officer interviewed shoplifters while waiting for uniformed police to arrive.

'A few questions, Eloise, that's all.'

'Anything I can do to help,' she said sweetly.

'Yes. Can you tell me if Richard Schumaker had a mobile phone?'

'Oh yes,' she replied promptly. 'He had it with him the day he was . . . he died.'

'We can't find it anywhere. It has disappeared,' he said, rubbing his chin. 'He definitely had it that day at the country club?'

'Oh yes. In fact, it rang twice during the meal.'

'Hmmm.'

That was strange, he thought. But he now drew one immediate conclusion: the murderer must have taken it. There was nobody else.

She nodded. 'I believe I fainted. I suppose it could have been taken while I was out.'

Angel pursed his lips.

'There's no other explanation,' he said pensively. 'You wouldn't know who phoned him, would you?'

'He didn't tell me. He just apologized, said it was work. He was polite, but he made it clear to the caller that the call was inconvenient, not welcome.'

'But you've no idea who rang?'

'None. Sorry.'

'Did you ever phone him?'

He was thinking he could have the phone traced if he knew the number.

'No.'

'Did you ever go to his house?'

She shook her head.

'I didn't know where he lived, Inspector. He said it was close by.'

'No. No,' he said patiently. 'Did you know a girl called Tania?'

'Unusual name. No.'

He wrinkled up his nose. This was getting him nowhere.

'Did you know that you were the last entry on a list of girls' names, a list that was found in Richard Schumaker's pocket?'

Her eyes narrowed. She slowly shook her head.

'No, Inspector. No. I didn't. What was that about?'

'I really have no idea,' he lied. He felt no obligation to speak the truth to witnesses, particularly those who could, perhaps, be more forthcoming.

TEN

'Yes. Come in. I've been looking all over for you.'

Ahmed protested. 'I've been looking for you, sir. You were out all day yesterday and you were out earlier today.'

'Well I'm here now. Look lively. You've about as much sparkle as a midwife's bicycle lamp,' Angel growled. 'What did that estate agent's say? Who instructed them?'

'Yes, sir. Penberthy's. Apparently, according to Mr Penberthy, Richard Schumaker instructed them himself, just before Christmas, on Friday, 23 December. And they put up the "For Sale" sign at the house on Monday, 2 January.'

Angel sniffed.

'That was the day he died,' he muttered grimly. 'Must have done it in the morning, before he went to Frillies.'

'And I've found Doctor Bell. He is a psychiatrist at the General Hospital on Burton Road.'

Angel's face dropped.

'Don't like the sound of that. It's those sort of doctors that send you batty!'

Suddenly, out in the corridor there was a loud scream. Sounded like a woman or a girl. It was a very loud scream. Then another.

They both stared at the door.

'Better see what it is,' Angel said urgently, waving his hand.

He jumped up, pushed the swivel chair back and made for the door.

The screaming continued.

'Hurry up.'

Ahmed grabbed the doorknob.

Angel charged out into the corridor.

The cadet followed close behind.

At first there was no sign of anything or anybody. Four or five other office doors opened and anxious faces looked out. Then, from the female locker room a WPC backed out into the corridor. It was clear to see that it was WPC Leisha Baverstock again. She was holding her face with both hands, and, as she turned, Angel could see her big eyes were bigger than ever, her mouth was open and her lips were quivering.

Angel stood there, realization dawning on him. He rubbed a hand slowly over his leathery face. 'It's that ruddy mouse again, Ahmed!' he said, turning away. 'You'll have to catch it, Ahmed. You'll have to catch it!'

Ahmed's jaw dropped.

'I can't catch mice, sir,' he said pathetically.

Angel growled.

'Well, see what you can do for her. I must get on,' he added and headed back to his office.

The Nosy Parkers, hanging out of the offices, withdrew and closed their doors.

Angel stormed down the corridor and reconsidered the merits and demerits of having a station cat. He reached his office, closed the door and slumped in the swivel chair. He rubbed an earlobe between finger and thumb. He recalled that he had heard screams like that in a CCTV recording of a bank siege, where a robber had shot an assistant bank manager. He remembered the crack of the bullet and the horrific reactions of the man's wife on being told later. His mind then drifted into thinking about the Rossi family and then, inevitably, to Mrs Buller-Price. It was time he was giving her a ring.

He reached out for the phone and dialled a number.

'Is that Mrs Buller-Price? This is Inspector Angel of —'

'Oh, hello there, Inspector,' she said, clearly delighted to hear from him. 'How nice of you to call, and so unexpectedly.' She stopped suddenly. Her voice changed to one of serious concern. 'Oh dear!' she said sombrely. 'I think I know why you've called. You're going to tell me that I have to return my lovely new car?'

Angel smiled.

'Not at all. No. This is just a friendly . . . social call,' he lied. 'I am merely concerned that you, as a pillar of the community, have all that you require; a woman living on her own and working virtually at the top of a mountain, in these winter months, you know. . . .'

'You are waffling, Inspector,' she said shrewdly. 'What is it you want? Are you wanting some of my scones?'

He didn't reply.

'You are after this car, aren't you?'

'No. No. Is it running well?'

'Like a bird!'

'That's good. Yes. Good. Well now, you know where to reach me if you have any problems.'

'Mmmm. Thank you, Inspector, and if you ever feel like a cup of tea and a piece of my Battenberg, you know where you can reach me,' she countered.

'Goodbye,' he said and replaced the handset.

He screwed up his face as if he'd taken a dose of Fenning's Fever Cure. He drummed his fingers irritably on the desk top. Patience was not one of his virtues. He anxiously wanted the action to begin. Unfortunately, he was not the one with the initiative. That was in the hands of the female of the species.

It was almost four o'clock and winter gloom was creeping across the cold blue sky as Angel pulled up outside The Brambles and parked behind the SOCOs' white transit van. He got out of the car and, as he was locking the door, he noticed out of his eye corner several motionless figures in silhouette, standing in the front bay windows of the four neighbouring houses. The news that a dead body had been found in the house had obviously leaked out. He sighed.

Voices and movement from behind caught his attention. He turned round to see two men in white paper overalls walking briskly down the short drive carrying a stretcher. On it was a shapeless zipped up sack, secured by three blue canvas straps. The SOCOs stopped at the rear of the transit, which had its doors open and fastened back in readiness. They lowered the stretcher on to rails on tracks fastened to the vehicle's floor and slid the stretcher inside. They closed the doors, climbed into the cab, started the engine, switched on the side-lights and drove away.

Angel watched the van rumble to the end of the street, where its indicator lights flashed brightly in the crisp air, and it took the corner.

Doctor Mac in white overalls, cap and boots came out of the front door of the house carrying a black case.

Angel saw him and followed him to his car that was parked a little further up the street.

'Hi Mac. What you got?'

The doctor looked surprised under the white hat and looked back.

'Oh, it's you, Michael,' he said, unlocking his car boot. 'How is that eye of yours getting along?'

'It's all right, Mac. Tell me what you found then?'

'Not much. A dead woman, injuries to her throat, half-dressed, that's about it.'

'Murder?'

'Probably.'

'Any forensic?'

'Maybe,' Mac said, as he tossed in the case, dragged off the hat and began to strip off the paper overalls.

'Murder weapon?'

'None found.'

'How old was she?'

'Young.'

'Any ID?'

'There's a handbag at the scene; seems big enough to have yards of ID in it.'

Angel nodded agreeably. He hoped so. He hated to have a body that came unaddressed.

'Anything else?'

'Empty perfume bottle, clothes, some rubbish.'

Angel's eyebrows shot up. He liked the sound of that. There were usually good clues in honest, untouched rubbish.

'What sort of rubbish?'

Mac shrugged and said, 'Just rubbish.' He stepped out of the white boots into leather shoes, threw the used suit, hat and rubber boots into the boot. 'Excuse me, Michael,' he added quickly and brushed past him to the car door. He opened it, jumped into the driving-seat, lowered the window and started the engine. 'I'll let you know what I can tomorrow. I'll give you a ring.'

'Yes. Fine. What's the big hurry?' Angel asked.

'For one thing, I have had no lunch,' Mac replied irritably.

Angel pointed to the glove box. 'I thought it was in that bottle you keep in there?' he said with a grin.

Mac looked at him patiently and shook his head. He let in the clutch, revved the engine and pulled away.

Angel went through the gate, up the drive, past a uniformed constable on the door and into the house. The hall carpet was covered in white sheeting. He stepped into the centre of it. He immediately lifted his nose in dismay. The smell was as pungent as before, but no longer sweet. He wrinkled his nose.

He called up the stairs.

'Is DS Taylor up there?'

A man's head and shoulders appeared round the newel post at the top.

'Yes, sir.'

'Right,' Angel said. 'I'm coming up. I want some gloves.'

'You won't need them, sir. We've about finished in there.'

Angel reached the top of the stairs. Another SOCO came out of the bathroom and held the door open for him.

'Ta,' he said, as he stepped into the room.

It looked very different from the way he had seen it a week ago. A complete wall had been removed and the four big mirrors that had made up the partition were now standing in the bath propped against the tiles. The space opened up was seven feet by ten feet and about ten inches deep. The back of it was a red brick and mortar wall. There were two copper pipes set vertically at the far end of the area draped with cobwebs, near to them on bare floorboards was an empty perfume bottle shaped like a fountain with its fancy stopper at the side of it. At the end nearest the door was a suitcase, a handbag, a housecoat, some pale blue underwear edged with white lace and some screwed up colourful wrappers of some sort. These items were jumbled together under a layer of fresh grey building dust.

Angel turned to DS Taylor.

'Where was the body then?'

'Horizontal on her side, sir. Facing the wall. Arms over her head. Feet together, legs pointed towards the door.'

He wrinkled his nose.

'It'd be a tight squeeze?'

'Yes. The back of her head was jammed up against the mirror.'

'How was she dressed?'

'Just a nightdress. Bare feet.'

'Hmmm. Did you see any wounds?'

'No, sir.'

'Blood?'

'No.'

Angel rubbed his chin. Then he pointed to the suitcase, handbag and other items on the floor.

'Has this stuff been photographed and checked for prints?' he said, squatting and peering closely at the pile of personal effects. He particularly noted the handbag next to the two colourful screwed up wrappers or packets on the dusty floorboards.

'Photographed, but not yet checked for prints, sir.'

'Hmmm,' he muttered, and took a pencil out of his pocket and proceeded to lift away a lace frill that was overhanging the handbag. 'When it has,' he said. 'Let Ron Gawber have this stuff, all of it, urgently.'

'Right, sir,'

Angel then carefully pushed the handbag round through ninety degrees so that he could see the front of it clearly. The design of the clasp comprised two intertwined gold snakes. His mouth twitched unhappily. He knew that the body was that of Tania Pulman.

'Doctor Bell?' Angel enquired.

'Come in, Inspector,' a man in his twenties with a high-pitched voice squealed impatiently. He had a bushy black beard and black-rimmed spectacles. 'I understand it is police business. I can give you five minutes. I have a long list of patients to see this morning,' he added. He reached out for a small plastic tomato-shaped timer on the desk top and dexterously cranked it round to the figure five.

Angel's mouth tightened. His eyebrows lifted slowly as he looked down at the little man and then took in the little interview room with its plain white walls and Spartan furnishings, comprising of a desk, an upholstered sprung chair, and one other chair made up of wooden slats, where he surmised had sat many a miserable and reluctant backside.

'Well, sit down. Sit down,' the little doctor snapped.

Angel didn't sit down. He rubbed his chin hard and deliberately slowly.

'If my presence and timing here is inconvenient, Doctor,' he said heavily. 'I can close the clinic and we can adjourn to the police station where I assure you, you will be able to allocate plenty of uninterrupted time to assist me with my inquiries.'

The doctor looked into Angel's eyes. He

began to consider that he might have met somebody he would have to pay attention to.

Angel waited.

The little timer ticked away several seconds.

'It sounds serious. What is it, Inspector?' Bell said.

'Murder is serious,' Angel said heavily.

Doctor Bell's eyebrows shot up.

'Murder? Oh dear. Who is it? Is it one of my patients?'

'Richard Schumaker.'

The doctor's jaw dropped.

'Oh dear. Who has he murdered?'

'I didn't say he had murdered anybody.'

'Saw your car pull up, sir. Just back from the hospital?'

'Yes. Come in, Ron. Shut the door. Sit down. The doctor said that Schumaker suffered from BPD. Borderline Personality Disorder. It's a . . . an across-the-board description for people who have difficulty controlling their emotions.'

'You mean Schumaker was off his head?' Gawber said.

Angel hesitated.

'No. The doctor said not. It was just a quirk in his character. Gave him pills for it.

But neglected, he said, it could have been dangerous.'

'So it doesn't necessarily mean that he murdered Tania Pulman?'

Angel sighed.

'No. Well, we'll have to wait for the post mortem. As they're both dead, we might never find out what exactly happened. However, I think Tania's name was heavily crossed out on that list in Richard Schumaker's pocket because she was dead.'

'And that list was a list of the women that Schumaker had successfully seduced or, anyway, bedded. A sort of score card.'

Angel wrinkled up his nose. He was reluctant to agree, but that did seem to be the explanation. 'Yes.'

'Maybe Eloise Macdonald got off lightly, sir. Maybe the man who murdered Schumaker unwittingly saved her life?'

Angel rubbed his chin.

'Maybe she knows who the murderer is,' Angel said. 'If it was a current boyfriend, she'd want to conceal his identity.'

'She seemed keen on Schumaker, sir.'

'She was, or she gave me the impression she was. She was quite smitten by him. It would be difficult to believe that she'd dine with a prospective lover then tolerate having him murdered before her eyes by her regular boyfriend.'

Gawber nodded.

'And why would he wear a mask?'

'I don't know,' Angel said. 'It wouldn't be to hide his face from her, if she knew who he was and it wouldn't matter if Schumaker identified him. He was going to be dead anyway. Doesn't make sense.'

There was a pause.

'There's something we're missing here, Ron, and I can't put my finger on it. I wish we could find Schumaker's mobile?'

Gawber shook his head.

'We've looked everywhere, sir.'

'If only we knew the service he used or the number.'

'We only have Eloise Macdonald's word that he had a mobile.'

Angel blinked. He squeezed an earlobe between finger and thumb. Then he said, 'All young people have mobiles these days, don't they?'

Gawber shrugged.

'And there's the murder weapon,' Angel said. 'The blood-covered shirt and jeans, the missing coat, gloves . . .'

'They're not buried in the grounds. There were positively no fresh earth marks anywhere.'

Angel's jaw stiffened.

'This case is going to go down as one of the great unsolved murders of our time.'

There was a knock at the door.

'Yes? Come in.'

It was Ahmed. He was carrying a message form.

'What is it?' Angel said irritably.

'Just come down the wire, sir,' Ahmed said. 'Thought you'd be interested. The judge trying Rikki Rossi has just thrown the case out and discharged him.'

Angel's face dropped. Rossi was free again.

Ahmed passed the message form over to Angel.

'I thought you'd like to know what the judge said, sir?'

Angel wrinkled his nose, looked down at the paper and began to read it out loud.

'The judge also said — listen to this, Ron — that the very recent murder of a key witness might have brought about a very different result of the case. And he went on to say that no one should believe that they can make fools of the police and turn British justice on its head.'

'Strong stuff, sir,' Gawber said grimly.

'Aye,' Angel said, rubbing his chin hard.

Angel reckoned Twelvetrees was lucky to have been able to drag the case out for two days, but it now looked as if Gina Rossi and her corrupt family would be back in command again in the north of England.

Strawbridge's plan had failed miserably, but fortunately, Angel had ideas of his own.

He turned back to Ahmed.

'Thanks Ahmed. Now get me DI Waldo White of the FSU in Wakefield on the phone,' he said quietly.

Gawber and Ahmed pricked up their ears. They wondered why he was contacting the head of the local police artillery so apparently spontaneously. They exchanged glances.

He looked up and caught them in the act. He glared at Ahmed. 'Get on with it. Do it from your own office. Chop chop!' he snapped. 'And put him through here.'

'Right, sir,' Ahmed said and rushed out.

'I'll crack on, sir,' Gawber said.

He followed Ahmed out of the office and closed the door.

Angel slumped in the chair, sniffed, picked up the phone and dialled a number.

There was a click and a familiar voice said, 'Mallin. Traffic division.'

'Yes, Norman. Angel here.'

'Oh yes. Are you fully recovered, sir? I heard you took quite a beating.'

'I'm fine. It's nothing,' he gabbled. 'That

197

car,' he added heavily. 'The one brought in by Mrs Buller-Price.'

'Oh yes, sir,' Mallin affirmed enthusiastically.

'Just giving you notice, Norman. I expect the fireworks to begin anytime now.'

ELEVEN

'There's no doubt about it, sir. It *is* Tania Pulman,' DS Donald Taylor announced as he closed the door.

Angel pointed to the chair by his desk.

'Appearance, description, passport, everything fits,' the SOCO continued.

Angel sniffed. He had already deduced that.

'What else?'

'Nothing unusual in her luggage, sir, her handbag and so on. What you'd expect an upwardly mobile young woman to carry about with her. The suitcase contained only clothes, make-up and stuff like that. But everything of the very best.'

Angel sniffed again.

'Except these, sir,' Taylor said, producing two straightened out colourful bags from his inside pocket. The predominant colour was turquoise and they were about the size and style of potato crisp packets; they had the words Cheapos Lucky Bag in red printed across the middle, and were illustrated with animals, party hats, clowns; illustrations that would be presumed to appeal to children.

'Those two were found empty and screwed up on the floor in the cavity where the body was found.'

Angel nodded. He had seen them there. He knew what they were. He frowned as he picked them off the desk. They were the bags a woman had shown to him and spoken about at length when he had first visited the supermarket to interview Eloise Macdonald.

'Any prints on them?'

'Schumaker's, nobody else's.'

'Hmm. Right. Leave them with me. And ask Doctor Mac to let me know the cause of death as soon as he can, will you?'

'Right, sir.'

Taylor went out.

Angel looked at the paper bags and rubbed his chin. Whilst he couldn't see any direct connection between them and the death of Tania Pulman, Richard Schumaker, or anybody else, it seemed mighty curious that in a house that was as tidy and clean as a new pin, two discarded empty paper bags should be hidden away. One could well understand why a body might be concealed

200

in the case of foul play, but why empty paper bags? They could as easily have been dumped in the bin, burned or taken away and disposed of away from the house. There was nothing illegal in the possession of Cheapos Lucky Bags. They didn't contain drugs or counterfeit goods, or poison; they weren't stolen property; why should they receive such unusual attention?

There was a knock at the door.

'Come in,' he called.

The door opened. It was Gawber.

'Ah, Ron, just the man,' Angel said, 'The dead girl *is* Tania Pulman. Her parents ought to be told.'

Gawber hesitated; it was a job nobody wanted.

'I was waiting for confirmation before setting up a formal ID, sir. Kill two birds with one stone. But I haven't had cause of death, yet. The lass was a bit of a minor celebrity, an up-and-coming model. And, by the way, some of the newspapers are belly-aching for a statement.'

Angel blinked; then, rubbing his chin, he said, 'This news might make the front page of some of the nationals?'

'With a sort of glamour photograph, I'm sure it would, sir.'

'Right, crack on with it then,' he said with

a frown.

Gawber turned to go.

'Just a minute, Ron,' he called. 'I wonder if we can incorporate that release with an appeal, an appeal for a man with a skull and crossbones tattoo on the back of his hand? If we do get any response, we can check off the names against the list we found in Schumaker's pocket. We desperately need the public's help with this case. Also, we need to know of anybody else who has experienced this sort of formalized assault, you know, starting with the throwing of an empty lager can, the threats, the waving of the knife, the tattoo, the mask and so on.'

'I know what you mean.'

'You'll need a glamour photo of Tania Pulman.'

'There are some sexy studio shots of her among her stuff in the suitcase,' Gawber said, his face brightening. 'I'll get right on to it, sir,' he said and turned to leave.

Angel said, 'Have you seen these?' He pointed to the empty lucky bags on his desk.

Gawber reached out and picked one of them up. He turned it over and took in the illustrations.

'Yes. They're from Cheapos. Kids go mad on them.'

'Kids, yes. What would Schumaker be doing with them and why would he chuck them in the cavity to hide them?'

Gawber frowned and shook his head.

'Beats me, sir.'

Angel growled.

The truth was, Cheapos Lucky Bags were beginning to get on Angel's nerves. The things were on his mind morning, noon and night. While he was driving home in the car, during his evening meal, his breakfast, watching television, his mind was on the lucky bags. When he woke up in the morning, it was the first thing he thought of. He knew they had something to do with the murders, but what?

Eloise Macdonald showed Angel into the little interview room by the reception counter in Cheapos giant supermarket.

'Back again so soon, Mr Angel?'

He thought he detected a self-confidence in her that had not been there previously.

'One or two questions about Cheapos Lucky Bags,' Angel said lightly.

Her eyes opened wide. She shook her head.

'Lucky bags? Aren't you looking for the man that killed Richard, Mr Angel?'

'We are working on that, Eloise. Still working on that. Never fear.'

'I would have thought it would have had quite a priority over our lucky bags.'

Angel wouldn't be drawn. He identified a distinct change in her. He pursed his lips and nodded slightly.

'Please sit down,' she said.

When they were seated facing each other over the table, she said, 'You know, Mr Angel, as I think about it, the man that murdered Richard had a good look at me. He may come looking out for me. He said he knew me. He said that I had been his girlfriend, which wasn't at all true. I would know a man I had been out with, whether he was wearing a mask or not. But he may think that I can identify him and give him away to you.'

'I wish you would.'

'I wish I could!'

Angel shook his head.

'If you have the slightest inkling of who it might be, you should tell me.'

'I don't know him. Never seen him before. If I had, I would have told you. But, I tell you, sometimes at night, in the dark, walking home, I think about it. It makes me nervous. If I think someone is following me, I worry about it. I wait until I can get into a good light, with other people, and slow down and, of course, the person walks straight past me.'

'If he'd wanted you dead, Eloise, he would have done it before now!' he said to put her at ease.

'I hope you're right.'

'Be assured, I am. As a matter of fact, my interest in the lucky bags is directly associated with Richard Schumaker's murder. Two empty bags were found hidden in his house,' he said, taking them out of his pocket. 'Have you any idea how he might have come by them or what they were doing there?'

'I have no idea. Cannot think. Unless there are any children he was saving them for.'

'No. As far as we can find out, he was a bachelor; lived on his own.'

'But he did shop here, and everybody is entitled to them, Mr Angel. All customers have to do is buy fifty pounds' worth of groceries to be entitled to a lucky bag. What they do with them, of course, is entirely up to them.'

'Of course. Now I need to know what is in them.'

'Sweets and novelties and small toys, I don't know in detail. I can get you a list.'

'Please do. Are the contents always the same?'

205

'No. They vary according to availability and also, to some extent, the season.'

'What do you mean?'

'Well, last year, they put in tiny chocolate eggs, also some bags had pretty little chenille chicks for Easter. At Christmas, a Father Christmas mask and beard, and miniature models of reindeer, dinosaurs, Mickey Mouse transfers, as well as sweets, perhaps a liquorice item, a party blow-out, a whistle, a party hat, a small toy and so on.'

'Hmmm. I need a few unopened bags and a list of contents.'

'You want to see me, sir?' Angel said, his head round the door.

'Yes,' Strawbridge growled. 'Come in. Sit down.'

Angel could see by the look on his face that the superintendent was about as happy as a dog in a desert.

'You'll have heard the news?'

'About Rossi?'

The corners of Strawbridge's mouth turned further downwards.

'Yes. He's been released. All charges dropped.'

Angel nodded grimly. 'It was inevitable as soon as Grady's body was found.'

Strawbridge jumped to his feet.

'*It doesn't make acceptance any easier!*' he bawled and pointed a finger at him. 'I want to make something quite clear to you, Angel. If your personal, private snout comes up with anything that will help me bottle Rikki Rossi, I want to know about it. Straightaway. Understand?'

'Right, sir,' Angel said, but there was a big fat zero's chance of him telling the superintendent anything that Helpman (or any other source) might provide in connection with that family of murderers, if it didn't precisely suit Angel's plans. An idea was well in hand for dealing with the Rossis, and the fewer people that knew about it, the better chance of its success.

Strawbridge settled back down in the swivel chair; he wiped his perspiring neck with his handkerchief; opened the middle drawer in his desk, threw a ruler into it noisily and slammed it shut. With a shaking hand, he stuffed the handkerchief roughly into his top pocket and then turned back to Angel.

'How are you getting on with that Schumaker case?'

'Difficult, sir. Difficult.'

'Of course it's difficult,' he snarled. 'If it was easy, they'd employ chimpanzees to do it and pay them in bananas! That's why you're paid big money.'

The skin on the back of Angel's hands tightened. He didn't consider that his salary could be described as 'big money'.

'So tell me about it,' Strawbridge said icily.

Angel blinked.

'Well, we have a witness who saw the murderer — rather close up, as it happens — and insists that he had a tattoo of a skull and crossbones on the back of his hand. CCTV shows that only three men seemed to be in the building at the time of the murder; none of them has the qualifying tattoo. I am hoping that the newspapers will help us to find the man. Also the body of a misper, Tania Pulman was found hidden in Richard Schumaker's house. It isn't yet clear how she died; I am awaiting the PM report, on her.'

'Anything else?'

'Lots of details, sir. There's the strange performance of the murderer before he actually stabbed the victim.'

'I've read it. That account from a witness?'

'Yes. Eloise Macdonald. Young woman in her twenties, works at Cheapos.'

'And you only have her word for it?'

Angel nodded.

'There's a missing mobile phone, isn't

there? The victim's?'

'We think so.'

Strawbridge frowned and shook his head. 'What do you mean?'

'Well, she's the only one who saw the mobile phone. The victim was said to have used it in her presence. Nobody else saw it or can throw any light on it.'

'Where is it now?'

'We don't know. The girl said she was unconscious — she fainted — when the murder was taking place. It is presumed that the murderer stole it while she was out. It was the manager of the club who woke her up.'

'And he's one of the three men, the suspects, in the building, I assume?'

'Yes. Martin Tickell. The other two are, Walter Flagg, the chef, and Louis Dingle, a waiter.'

'Nothing known, I suppose.'

'Clean sheet. All of them.'

'What are your lines of inquiry?'

'I am following up the peculiar situation of two empty lucky bag packets found hidden in Richard Schumaker's house.'

Strawbridge stared at him with piercing small eyes.

'Can't see what lucky bag packets have to do with a murder.'

It would be difficult trying to explain. In the mood he was in Angel wasn't even going to try.

'Not certain, myself, sir. Also, there's a missing coat from the cloakroom at the club; I am assuming it was taken by the murderer to cover his blood-stained clothes.'

'Hmmm. Doesn't that suggest that the murderer left the premises immediately after killing Schumaker?'

'It's possible, sir. But if he did, he would have to leave by the kitchen delivery door to avoid the CCTV on the main doors. Any such person would have been seen possibly by the waiter, and almost certainly by the chef who was in there preparing for a big function that night. Of course, they are both possible suspects themselves, anyway.'

'Hmmm. So, what are you doing about it, then?'

'Routine inquiries. Leg work. Checking on everything.'

'You don't know what you are doing, do you?' Strawbridge said, his wet lips grinning in a strange sort of way. 'You are dragging this case out, hoping that something will turn up.'

Angel's face went scarlet; his lips tightened. 'I know *exactly* what I am doing, sir. And I'll have this solved and passed on a plate to the CPS while you're still . . .' He stopped. If he had continued and said what was really on his mind, he would have been drummed out of the force.

'While I'm still what?' Strawbridge said heavily.

'While you are still the Detective Superintendent here at Bromersley,' Angel said smoothly.

'Right. Yes. I am that. I am, and don't you forget it.'

Angel parked his car under the portico at Frillies Country Club, behind a tractor which had a low trailer hooked to it. On the trailer were twelve dustbins with metal lids on the tops resting at various angles.

As he pulled himself out of the car, an unpleasant smell assaulted his nostrils and he looked curiously at the vehicle and its load.

A scruffy, bearded man smothered in an old army greatcoat, a scarf, thick gloves and Wellington boots strode animatedly out of Frillies' front door immediately followed by the manager, Martin Tickell. The man in khaki was waving his hands all over, in an agitated manner. Tickell had an unhappy face, appeared to be saying nothing and avoided looking directly at the man.

'The vet's bill alone will be over a hundred pounds!' the man bawled out in a crisp Welsh accent you could slice leeks with. 'Where do you think I am going to get that from, boyo? Eh? Come over here. I show you.'

The man went up to the trailer, reached over to a dustbin at the rear of it and whisked off the lid. He glared back at Tickell and said, 'There! Look you, in there!'

Tickell tried to see inside the bin without moving towards it.

Angel couldn't resist his curiosity and approached the two men. Tickell noticed him for the first time and passed a hand across his mouth in embarrassment.

'Oh, Inspector Angel! Did you want to see me?'

The Welshman looked up.

'Inspector, did you say? Inspector of what?' he asked gruffly.

'I am a police inspector, what's the trouble exactly?'

'It is nothing. We can sort it out,' Tickell said, looking from one to the other.

'I'll tell you, Mr Inspector,' the Welshman said loudly. 'I buy throw-out food from these premises. I pay a good price for food for my pigs, for edible waste. Edible, mark you! What did I get the other day, but a raincoat complete with buttons! Plastic buttons. What sort of nourishment is that for pigs, I ask you? One of my piglets ate some of it and is mighty sick. Now I have to decide whether to put it down or not. And, to boot, I have to pay a veterinary's fee as long as your arm.'

Angel's eyebrows shot up.

'Is the raincoat in there?' he asked, pointing to the dustbin.

'And what a tattered mess it is, yes! That's evidence, isn't it, Mr Inspector? That's proof positive.'

'Can I see it? Will you pull it out for me?'

The Welshman eagerly pulled up his coat-sleeve and pulled out a khaki, sludgy mess, which he shook several times to unfurl and it slowly was revealed to be the remnants of a man's grey raincoat with a huge hole torn out of the front. He draped it over the other bins in the trailer.

'Can you see if there is a label in the back of the neck.'

The smell of ammonia began to have an effect on Angel's eyes. He pulled back from the trailer.

The Welshman found the shop's logo and read it out.

'It just says Challender's. What difference does that make, boyo?'

Angel wiped his eyes with a handkerchief.

'Anything in the pockets?' he muttered through the linen.

'I never looked, you know,' the Welshman said, his eyebrows shooting upwards. 'I never looked.' He ferreted away and eventually waved a yellow glove in the air.

'Ah,' Angel declared. 'Is there one in the other pocket?'

The man did some more ferreting and produced the other.

There was no doubt about it: it *was* the missing raincoat.

'I'll have to take the coat as evidence, sir,' Angel said to the Welshman. 'Can you tell me how you came by it.'

Tickell moved his hand from across his mouth and nose and said, 'The missing raincoat, Inspector. Of course.'

Angel nodded at him.

The Welshman noticed the exchange, rubbed his beard and said, 'I leave my bins here at the rear, of course, and the kitchen staff fill them with any left-over food that must be edible, naturally. I collect the full bins usually every day, swop them over for empty bins. And I settle up every month with this man here, Martin Tickell.'

Angel nodded.

'When did you collect the bin which, you

214

say, had the raincoat in it?'

'I don't know,' he said jeeringly. 'And it did have the raincoat in it. All I know is that I have a mighty sick piglet and this coat was being dragged round the sty by another of them.'

Angel shook his head.

The Welshman saw him and suddenly roared, 'Here! What am I doing involving the police? I don't want the judiciary involved in this. I'm doing nothing wrong. I just want compensation. What's right, you know. That's all.'

'That's all right,' Angel said. 'Have you come across anything else that . . . well, shouldn't have been there in the bins?'

He rubbed his beard again.

'No. Once found a soup ladle in and among.'

Angel made a decision. He dug into his pocket, pulled out his mobile and dialled a number. There was a click and it was answered.

'I want SOCO. Is that Don Taylor?'

Angel organized the immediate searching of the Welshman's trailer, his food stores, his pig sties, and the bins at the rear of Frillies. He told the reluctant farmer that his vehicle must stay where it was until the bins on the trailer had been searched.

Angel's intervention in the dispute between Tickell and the Welshman had strangely subdued the farmer and brought the two men together. They retired to Tickell's office quietly, no doubt to settle the matter over a pot of tea.

A few minutes later, the SOCOs' van arrived. Angel instructed DS Taylor and a DC who immediately began examining the trailer and its contents. He then made his way through to the restaurant and into the kitchen where young Walter Flagg was checking his cooking in one of the big gas-fired ovens. He was in his whites and traditional chef's hat. Perspiration was running down his face.

Flagg glanced across at the door, then back at the oven. 'Hello there, inspector. I'm very busy. Big do tonight again. Masonics. Two staff off with flu.'

'There's a man at the front, a Mr Davies . . .'

'Yapping about his sick pig, I know. I know,' he said without looking back. 'I've had it all morning. Don't know how the coat got into the pigswill, though. I'm not necessarily convinced it came from here. He might have picked it up at some of his other calls. I know he collects from The Feathers, in town.'

Angel pursed his lips.

'No. No. It came from here all right. Will you show me where the bins are kept?'

Flagg nodded. He closed the oven and made for the back door of the kitchen, down two steps, then to a small lean-to outhouse. The door was wide open. He pointed at it. Angel peered inside. There were four bins lined up against the wall.

'There,' Flagg said, indicating them.

'Is this door open all the time?'

'It's locked at night.'

'Who's got the key?'

'I have one and Martin Tickell has one.'

'You lock it every night?'

'Yes,' he said firmly. 'Want to see any more?'

'No.'

They went back into the kitchen.

Flagg moved straight across to another oven and opened the door.

'Yes, but who had access the day of the murder?'

'I can't remember now specifically, but everybody, I suppose,' he said, reaching up for a big spoon to baste the meat.

'Who's everybody? You, I suppose. The waiter fellow, Louis Dingle, and the manager Martin Tickell.'

'Yes, and the others who work here in the

kitchen and those who serve in the restaurant and the bar of an evening. Part-timers, you know.'

Angel sniffed and rubbed his chin.

'Have you a mobile phone, Mr Flagg?'

'Yes, of course. Hasn't everybody?' he said throwing the spoon in the sink and closing the oven door.

'Can I see it?'

Flagg frowned.

'Of course.'

He turned towards a bank of lockers at the far end of the kitchen, opened the first one, reached into a pocket in a coat hanging in there and handed it to him.

Angel hardly glanced at it and handed it back.

'Thank you. Had it long?'

'A couple of years . . . what's all this about?'

Angel made a face that was supposed to be a reassuring smile.

'It's all right. Where's Mr Dingle?'

'He'll be around in the restaurant or the bar or the cellar.'

'Thank you very much.'

He pushed the swing door back into the restaurant.

'Good luck, inspector,' Walter Flagg called after him.

Angel wrinkled up his nose in response then shook his head. He had been telling himself that luck had nothing to do with it. Now, he wasn't so certain.

He looked round the restaurant. All the tables were set and the glass and silver glinted on the crisp white tablecloths. He heard bottles rattling accompanied by heavy breathing from behind the bar.

Angel ambled over to it.

'Hello. Anybody there?'

A face came up between beer pump handles. It was Louis Dingle.

'Ah. Inspector Angel, what can I do for you, sir?'

'A few questions.'

He was in his white shirt and black trousers, bow tie, with his coat draped across the back of the chair at the nearest table.

'Phew! I could do with a rest. Let's sit down a minute.'

Dingle came from behind the bar, strode over to the table, pulled out a chair and sat down.

'I've been at it all morning. I'm fair whacked.'

Angel pulled out a chair and sat opposite him.

'What can I do for you, Inspector? I take it you haven't found the murderer yet?'

'No. Not yet.' He sighed, pursed his lips and said, 'Just a few bits and pieces to tie up,' he said misleadingly. He always believed in conveying the impression to suspects and parties directly involved that detection of the guilty was only a matter of time and diligence. He licked his lips slowly and said, 'Richard Schumaker's young lady, Eloise Macdonald, said that his mobile phone rang on two occasions during the meal, that he answered it and spoke for a little while each time. Did you see him speaking on a mobile at all while you were serving them?'

Dingle seemed perplexed at this question. He looked down at the table in front of him and moved a fork about a tenth of an inch as if it was out of position, and then he moved it back again. He shook his head and looked up at him.

'I'm sorry, Inspector. I don't actually recall seeing him with a mobile phone. Wasn't there one found in his pocket?'

'That's the funny thing, Mr Dingle. No phone was found on him or anywhere in the conservatory either. I was thinking, he didn't leave it by any chance in here, did he? Didn't fall out of his pocket or . . . ?'

'I didn't see him with a phone, or speaking on a phone. Of course, I was in and out. He could have. I didn't find a phone.

Nobody handed a phone in. Sorry, can't help there.'

'Do you have a mobile?'

'Yes. Of course.'

'Had it long?'

'About a year,' he said and pulled it out of his trouser pocket.

Angel glanced at it and nodded.

'There's a man who collects food for his pigs.'

Dingle pulled a face. 'Mr Davies. Yes. I heard. He says a coat was dumped in one of the bins from here.'

'Yes. I wondered if you could explain how the coat got into the pigswill?'

'No idea.'

Angel shook his head again. Nobody knew anything about anything. He pursed his lips.

'Well, if an explanation occurs to you, perhaps you'll let me know.'

'Sure thing, Inspector.'

Angel stood up.

'Thank you.'

'Good luck, Inspector.'

Angel stared at him then growled something under his breath. The second word was *off,* and the first word sounded like sugar, but was not as sweet.

He made his way out of the restaurant, down the plush corridor to reception and tapped the bell on the counter.

Martin Tickell came through the archway still looking ill at ease. 'Oh it's you, Inspector. What now?'

'Where's your farmer friend?'

'He's gone, and he's no friend of mine. He's expecting the club to pay his vet's bills. I have agreed to put it before the grand council, but there's no chance of that, I can tell you. Have your men finished here? Members don't like police around; gives the club a bad name.'

'That's tough,' Angel said irritably. 'We're going to be here as long as it takes, so you'd better get used to it.'

Tickell licked his lips nervously; maybe he had spoken too brusquely. He didn't reply.

'Do you have a mobile phone?'

'Can't be without it in this business,' he said, pulled it out of his pocket and waved it at the inspector.

Angel nodded his acknowledgement.

'When Richard Schumaker and his young lady came to lunch, did you see him use a mobile phone at all, in the restaurant or anywhere?' Angel said stiffly.

'I don't think so. I don't really remember. But I don't like people using them in the restaurant. If I had been in there, and he was using it, I would definitely have noticed.'

Angel wrinkled his nose. Maybe Schumaker didn't have a mobile; only Eloise Macdonald seemed to have seen it.

TWELVE

Angel threw his coat at the hook on the cabinet and missed. He grunted something improper and bent down to pick it up. He found the loop at the back of the neck and hung it properly on the hook. He looked down at the pile of envelopes and reports on his desk and slumped down in the swivel chair.

He reached out for the phone and dialled a number. It rang out for about half a minute. He grunted impatiently, cancelled it and dialled a different number. That was answered promptly.

'Cadet Ahaz. You wanted me, sir?'

'Ahmed, where's the super? He isn't in his office.'

'Don't know, sir. Sorry.'

'Right.'

Angel replaced the phone and leaned back in the chair. He had not been able to contact Strawbridge all day. It was unusual for a superintendent to be inaccessible for any length of time without some info filtering down as to where he was. If it was illness, a meeting, a course or holidays, a temporary chain of authority was always set up. Nobody had said anything to him. He thought it was strange, like a train puffing along without a driver.

There was a knock at the door and Gawber's head popped through. 'You wanted me, sir?'

Angel brightened.

'Yes. Come in, Ron. Sit down. Haven't seen the super lately, any idea what he's up to?'

Gawber shook his head.

'S'funny. DI Asquith asked me the same question, sir. Nobody's seen him.'

Angel shrugged.

'I have just got back from Frillies.' He sniffed. 'Nobody *saw* anything. Nobody *knows* anything. Everybody was asleep. I might as well be talking to an emu in Urdu. There are too many gaps. Too many things we don't know. Somebody is making a monkey out of me and I don't like it.'

Gawber sighed.

'I was thinking, sir, you know nobody has seen this murderer, only Eloise Macdonald. Nobody has seen Schumaker's mobile, only

Eloise Macdonald. And at the vital time, just after the actual stabbing by the murderer, Eloise Macdonald is unconscious, she says, in a faint.'

'Yes. I had noticed.'

'Convenient, isn't it?'

Angel rubbed his neck.

'We've had some pretty good liars through our hands, Ron, over the years.'

Gawber nodded. They certainly had.

'I don't know,' Angel said.

Gawber said, 'The more guilty they are, the bigger liars they are.'

'True. True. But one of those three men at the club, Tickell, Flagg or Dingle has to be our murderer, unless Eloise Macdonald is flying under false colours and she knows something we don't.'

'If she's a liar, sir, the murderer could be anybody. Do you want to have her in, and go through her statement again?'

'Not yet. Not unless we have something we can spring on her, shake her up a bit. Unnerve her. You know what I mean.'

The phone rang. He reached out for it.

'Angel. Yes?'

It was Doctor Mac.

Angel's face brightened.

'Now then, Michael, I've finished the PM on that lass, Tania Pulman.'

'Ah,' Angel said enthusiastically. 'Good of you to ring, Mac. What have you got?'

'Aye, well, she has contusions on the throat, consistent with her being choked by a person with large hands — that would be any adult male, really — causing asphyxiation and inhibiting the supply of blood to the brain, resulting in death. Her fingernails were freshly damaged so she put up some resistance, not a lot, I would think. Died whilst on her back, possibly during sexual activity or just afterwards, and left in that position twenty-four to forty-eight hours before being moved and lodged on her left side for approximately twenty days. Lungs bone dry. No signs of any poison, drugs or alcohol — unusual these days — but semen from Richard Schumaker was found on her and her clothing.'

'No needle marks, tattoos, body-piercing?'

'Nothing like that, Michael.'

Angel nodded.

'Right. Thanks for ringing it through, Mac. Is she fit to be seen for ID?'

'She will be, in, say an hour.'

'I'll have somebody from the family drop by. Thanks again, Mac. Goodbye.'

Angel cancelled the call by depressing the cradle, but he kept hold of the receiver and dialled a number.

He caught Gawber's eye.

'He confirms it was Richard Schumaker. She was choked to death whilst on her back and left there for at least twenty-four hours, presumably during or after sexual intercourse.'

Gawber blinked.

'Sounds like something dippy a young lunatic would get up to for kicks.'

Angel heard a voice in the phone.

'Cadet Ahmed Ahaz, sir.'

'Yes, Ahmed. Find DS Crisp for me, pronto.'

'Right, sir.'

He replaced the phone.

Gawber said, 'So we have one murder solved.'

'That's the easy one.'

Gawber sighed.

'What do you want me to do now, sir?'

Angel thought for a moment and then said, 'I think we'll ask for the assistance of our friends in the media.' He spoke sarcastically. 'We didn't get any useful replies to that glamour photo of Tania Pulman in the national papers, did we?'

'A lot of cranks, sir. That's all.'

'Run it again. Change the photograph. Give them something even more daring to look at. Say that her body has been found and add a supplementary inquiry. Tell them we are looking for a man in his twenties. Tell them about the tattoo, the knife, the lager can, the dancing about, annoying a courting couple and so on. See if we can pull anything in with that: there may be a few girls who have had a near miss with Richard Schumaker.'

The phone rang. He reached out for it.

'Angel.'

'DS Taylor, sir. SOCO.'

'Yes Don?'

'We've been very thoroughly through Mr Davies's pig sties, all of his bins, his trailer, his Land-Rover and his food store sir. A rotten job, sir, I can tell you.'

Angel agreed that it certainly would have been. He sensed there was something of interest coming.

'What did you find?' he said attentively.

'Blood-stained shirt and jeans among mud in one of Davies's pig sties.'

Angel's face brightened.

'Great.'

'And stuck to the bottom of one of the bins in slime, some torn up pieces of a photograph, sir. I am pretty certain it is of that model, Tania Pulman.'

Angel's pulse began to bang in his ears.

'Yeah!'

'And two empty Cheapos Lucky Bags, sir.'

Angel felt the excitement of a 3-year-old on Christmas Eve.

'That's good. The net is closing, Don. Let me have the bits of the photograph and the lucky bags as soon as you've done with them.'

'Right, sir.'

'Thanks Don,' he said and returned the phone to its cradle. His eyes glistened briefly.

'What is it, sir?' Gawber said eagerly.

Angel explained excitedly what the SOCO had found.

Gawber nodded and said, 'What about the DNA, sir?'

Angel sighed and pulled a face.

'More likely to get the DNA of Miss Piggy, than the murderer's!'

It was as black as a Barnsley pit chimney and as cold as a pit pony's nose.

The church clock had struck 4 a.m.

Angel was in bed fast asleep next to his beloved Mary when the raucous, tinny jangle of the mobile phone on the bedside table disturbed the cold quiet of the night. He woke easily and reached out quickly for the bedside light switch. Then he snatched up the persistent phone and pressed the

230

button before the noise disturbed his wife.

'Yes?' he whispered.

'Is that DI Angel?'

'Yes.'

'DC Tallow, sir, Traffic Division. Sorry to bother you. DS Mallin has put a flag on a tracer here to contact you on this number if there is any movement of a particular vehicle.'

'Yes. That's quite right.'

'Well, sir. That vehicle has moved from its regular stationary place at Tunistone and is moving in a westwardly direction, over the Pennines.'

'How far has it travelled?'

'About ten miles, sir.'

'Hmmm. Right. Will you advise me when it stops moving and comes to rest for more than an hour? Then I'll want an exact location.'

'I will, sir.'

'Thank you. Goodnight.'

'Goodnight, sir.'

He cancelled the phone, switched off the light and pulled the blankets back over his head. There was about as much chance that he would get back to sleep as there was of Robert Mugabe becoming the Prime Minister of England.

■ ■ ■ ■

It was 8.28 a.m.

Angel was making his way down the station corridor. He heard a phone ringing out. He realized it was the phone in his office. His jaw tightened and he increased his pace. He reached the office, pushed open the door, reached over the desk and snatched it up.

'Angel,' he bawled into the mouthpiece.

It was the civilian telephonist on the station exchange.

'Oh. Good morning, Inspector,' she said coolly. 'There's a Mrs Buller-Price on the line for you. I don't know whether you want to speak to her or . . .' She tailed off.

'Of course I do,' he replied sharply. He didn't like the way the receptionist wanted to filter his calls. He made it a policy to speak to every caller who asked for him by name: he soon gave them short shrift if he discovered they were wasting his time. On this occasion, he had been expecting to hear from the dear lady, and he knew exactly what she was going to say. 'Put her through, please.'

There was a click and the familiar voice began, 'Oh, Inspector Angel, I'm so terribly sorry to trouble you,' she said, sounding worried.

'That's all right, Mrs Buller-Price,' he said gently.

'But it's my new car,' she wailed. 'Well, the car that was somehow left to me. I never did quite understand all the innings and outings. It's been taken! Stolen in the night. I came in from the stable a few minutes ago and, lo and behold, it had gone. It was there last night at six o'clock. Clearly somebody has, erm, taken it.'

'Oh,' Angel said, trying to sound surprised. 'I'm very sorry to hear that, Mrs Buller-Price. And I will certainly look into it straight away. But tell me, are you without transport now entirely?'

'Now, there's a funny thing, Inspector,' she said. 'A very funny thing. I think that Mr Lestrange — you will remember he is the gentleman who was repairing my Bentley for me — Mr Lestrange told me only last Monday that he was now in possession of the engine part that was needed to repair the car, so it *is* possible that he could have it running for me very soon.'

'Good. Good.'

'And I am not entirely certain that that lovely new car was really intended for me, you know, Inspector. I mean morally. I hadn't done anything to earn or deserve it, so I have never been quite comfortable about owning it, if you see what I mean.'

Angel thought the conversation was going rather well; it coincided beautifully with plans already afoot.

'Well, let's see if I can recover the car first,' he said cautiously. 'We have its description, index number, on file, so leave it with me.'

'Of course, I'm very happy to do that, Inspector. And, in the meantime, I'll see if I can jolly dear Mr Lestrange along, to get my old bus back on the road today.'

'That seems to be an excellent course of action, Mrs Buller-Price.'

'Do you know, Inspector,' she said in a confidential tone, 'I do so look forward to getting behind the wheel of it again. You know, there's a lot more room in a Bentley than in that posh new car! The steering is easier too. And the leather upholstery . . .'

Angel smiled.

'Good. Good. Now, if I'm able to recover the car, I'll be in touch with you immediately.'

'On reflection, I don't think I will want it back now, not if I can get my Bentley repaired.'

'Well, we'll see. Take care now. But if it doesn't work out, and you are without any transport, do let me know.'

'Well, thank you. Thank you, Inspector. Thank you very much and goodbye.'

He replaced the phone and pursed his lips. He thought that that tête-à-tête had passed rather well. He hoped that the Bentley could be safely repaired for her use. After all, it was possible he might not recover the new car and he wouldn't have been happy knowing that dear Mrs Buller-Price, living half-way up the Pennines, working a farm on her own, at her age, was stranded without any suitable transport.

There was a knock at the door.

It was Gawber wearing a smile and waving a newspaper.

'Good morning, sir,' he said brightly as he closed the door.

'Come in. Good morning, Ron.'

'Seen the papers? It's on the front page of most of them. The *Daily Examiner* has done us proud. Blown up photograph of her and the full story!'

Angel sniffed.

'Sit down,' he said. 'I've seen it. They've only published it on the front page because her nipples practically poke your eyes out.'

Gawber smiled.

'It's got us what we wanted, sir.'

'We'll see,' Angel said quietly. He eased

back on the swivel chair, looked closely at him as he rubbed his chin. 'I've got a job for you, Ron. Last night, I had an idea. Don't you think if Schumaker had a mobile phone, that his father would know the number?'

Gawber thought about it for a moment.

'But his father's dead, sir.' Then his eyes flickered, showing that he was thinking. Realization dawned on him. 'It would likely be in the father's phone's memory though, or his address book, wouldn't it?'

Angel nodded.

'Hopefully.'

There was a knock at the door.

'Come in,' Angel called, then turned back to Gawber. 'Well, crack on with that, then. Phone Liverpool Central, speak to DI Callahan . . .'

It was DS Crisp at the door.

'Come in.'

Gawber nodded to him as he dashed out of the room.

Crisp closed the door.

Angel glared at him.

'Where've you been? On your holidays? I told Ahmed I wanted you yesterday afternoon.'

'I've been very busy, sir. There was a stream of enquiries at the desk about that model, Tania Pulman.'

'What sort of enquiries?'

'Well, all sorts of people wanted to know her address, who she had worked for, details like her age, and the address of her parents.'

'You didn't give any info like that out, I hope?' he bawled.

'Oh no, sir.'

'Has anything useful come out of it, then?'

'I don't think so, sir. It's in my report.'

Angel shook his head. His reports were always very readable, as readable as the Brothers Grimm and just about as believable. He didn't suppose that Crisp had been wholly occupied the entire day on such a cause, but, as usual, he couldn't check on it.

'Well, it's going to be even busier in that regard. At least I hope it is. Among the interest and questions you may have to field today about Tania Pulman's murder, I want you to listen up for a female: somebody, *anybody,* who thinks they know Richard Schumaker, has had the experience of being courted, escorted, taken out, made love to, whatever the modern euphemism is, by him. Got it?'

'Yes, sir.'

'Crisp,' Angel said pointedly. 'We need a bit of luck.'

'Right, sir.'

'Before that,' he said patiently. 'I've a job for you. It's still to do with that lass. We need formal ID. An awful job. Will you see to it? I suppose it will have to be her parents.'

Crisp didn't react.

'Right sir,' he said promptly, got up and made for the door.

'And Crisp,' Angel said.

The sergeant turned back.

'Yes sir?'

'Be gentle about it. It's an awful thing for parents. . . .'

'Oh I will, sir,' he said earnestly.

The door closed.

Angel rubbed his chin. He was wondering whether he should have done the job himself. He usually did IDs, particularly when the relationship was close and therefore potentially distressing, but the enemy today was time.

He must check and see what was happening to Mrs Buller-Price's car.

He reached out for the phone and dialled a number.

'DS Mallin.'

'It's Michael Angel, what's happening to that car?'

'Ah, yes sir. It is presently travelling up

Bury New Road in Manchester. It has made three stops at addresses in the city for varying lengths of time, but not longer than an hour. It has also stopped briefly, I think it was probably for fuel, on Cheetham Hill Road. None of these stops were for more than an hour, so I didn't advise.'

'Quite right. Quite right. Keep watching it closely.'

'Do you want me to advise Manchester police to assist, sir?'

Angel's heart missed a beat.

'No, no,' he bawled. 'Definitely *not*. This is a highly covert operation. I don't want you to tell anybody, and I do mean *anybody!*'

The emphasis was not lost on Sergeant Mallin.

'Didn't know it was like that, sir.'

'Oh yes. Most important.'

'Right, sir.'

Angel replaced the phone. He thought for a moment then smiled and rubbed his hands like a fishmonger on Maundy Thursday. Everything was going beautifully to plan.

THIRTEEN

Angel looked up from the report he was reading.

'Yes?'

It was Ahmed.

Angel noted that his eyes were shining and he was wearing a grin.

'There's a young lady in reception, sir,' he said eagerly. 'Says she knew the murdered man. Actually went out with him.'

Angel blinked. A witness at last.

'Ah!' he said. 'Right. Show her into an interview room. Is there one free?'

'I'll check, sir.'

He dashed off.

Angel stood up and watched the door close. He licked his lips. He had to stop himself getting too excited at the arrival of someone who *said* she was a witness and who *might* be able to provide evidence to resolve this case. He had been disappointed before.

He gathered together the letters and reports he had been wading through into a neat pile and pushed it to the corner of the desk. He rubbed his chin. He reckoned he was due for a break. It was time this nonsensical mystery was solved and the murderer caught. This could be the pivotal point. He pulled out a new cassette from the cupboard behind him, rushed out of the room and down the corridor. He peered through the glass panel in the door of interview room number one, and saw a foursome round a table. He sniffed and moved away. Interview room number two was vacant. He pushed open the door, switched on the recorder, pushed a cassette in the slot, then dashed over to the window, opened it and set the arm on the first notch. Then he heard the hard crack of high-heeled shoes on red tiles galumphing down the corridor. His timing was perfect. He went to the door. There was Ahmed and a pretty young woman.

Ahmed coughed and then said, 'This is Miss Mirabelle Jones, sir.'

Angel smiled across at her.

'Come in, Miss Jones.'

The young lady came into the room looking round at the walls, the desk and then at Angel.

He turned to Ahmed.

'You'd better stay, lad.'

Ahmed closed the door.

He glanced at the young, fresh-faced girl in her twenties. She was bright eyed and had tidy brown hair. She was wearing a light-coloured raincoat, unbuttoned to show a grey jumper and a well-pressed navy blue skirt. She wore brown stockings and polished leather shoes with heels so high that she made loud clomps with every step. Her hands were fair skinned, free of jewellery and her nails were rounded as God intended and clear varnished. She carried a handbag in one hand and a compact umbrella in the other.

He nodded at her. He totally approved: here was a girl, for once, that looked like a girl!

'Please sit down. I'm Inspector Angel. What can I do for you?' he asked quietly, maintaining the smile.

'You are the officer dealing with the murder of that model, Tania Pulman, and that man, Richard Schumaker?' she said hesitantly.

'Yes.'

She shuddered. Then she looked at the chair for a second or so as if she was deciding whether to stay or not. She slowly lowered herself into it.

'I suppose what happened to her could have happened to me,' she said.

Angel's eyebrows shot up. He was looking forward to whatever she had to say.

Mirabelle Jones wrapped her coat over her knees and anchored it by placing the black leather handbag and umbrella on her lap.

'I've never been into a police station before,' she said, looking across the table at him. 'Never had a reason to.'

He pursed his lips and waited.

Mirabelle Jones seemed intelligent and was becoming less nervous by the second.

'I was told you knew the murdered man?' he said quietly, as he sat down opposite her.

'Yes, I did.'

'Do you mind if we record this interview? Saves time messing around taking notes.'

She nodded.

He pushed the cassette into the machine and pressed the red button.

'Interview with Miss Mirabelle Jones, 12 January, 10.36 a.m., present, DC Ahaz and DI Angel,' he gabbled as he checked that the spools were rotating.

He turned back to the girl.

'You knew the murdered man?'

'Not very well. Met him twice. Lovely man. I recognized his description and the business with the empty lager can, and the tattoo and the knife, from the newspaper this morning. In my case, Jason fought the man with the knife, disarmed him and scared him off. If he hadn't, he might have killed me like he did that model, Tania Pulman.'

Angel frowned.

'Who's Jason?'

'That's Richard Schumaker, I suppose. I knew him as Jason.'

Angel wrinkled his nose.

'Jason?'

There was a new name to conjure with.

'Jason was ever so brave and nice. Well, I thought he was. I don't know now. Doesn't make sense really. He just disappeared until this . . .'

He nodded attentively.

'Well, tell me what happened.'

She licked her lips.

'Don't know where to start. I was on a date with Jason. It was in the summer, July. I met him in The Feathers. I had called there for a drink after I had been shopping. It was my half-day. He'd bought me a port and lemon, without me noticing that he had noticed me, if you see what I mean. And we made a date for the same day, the following week. It was Saturday, 30 July, twelve noon at The Feathers. We had lunch and a bottle of wine, to get to know each other better, and, well, to take it from there. We then decided . . . well, *he* decided really, to walk up to the park. It was a lovely day. I expected him to have a car, but he said he liked to walk. We went in Jubilee Park, the top entrance, through the cricket field. It was a nice, warm day. We were talking about this and that. I was trying to find out what he did for a living and he sort of said — implied — that he didn't need to work, that his father was well off in some sort of profession, a solicitor or a doctor, I suppose he meant. Anyway, he said that his father funded him. Got a regular cheque. Very nice, I thought. I should be so lucky. But he was ever so nice. Anyway, there was a little rose arbour not far from the main gates. It's sort of through an arch of flowers at the end of a short winding path; it's very nice and quiet. We went there. There was a bench and we sat down on it. It was warm, so he took his coat off. He put his arm round me and we chatted for a while. I thought he was going to kiss me. He might have done, but he didn't, because, next thing, an empty tin can came flying through the air and landed at our feet. It startled me, I can tell you. Then a tall young man in a dark shirt and jeans, and a tattoo of a skull and crossbones on the back of his left hand, leapt out from behind some bushes. He stood there, waving a huge knife around in the air. He made some remark that I was *his* girl and that Jason should leave me alone. That I was his. But I had no idea who he was. I had never seen him in my life before, or since, nor do I want to. He then challenged Jason and made to stab him with the knife. Jason leapt up immediately and tried to take the knife off him. He made some frightening sort of lunges towards him. I was terrified!'

Angel nodded agreeably. This evidence was fitting in beautifully with what was already known. It showed great promise. He must keep her talking.

'Then what happened?'

'I, erm, naturally looked round to see what way I could help him. There was nothing handy I could have used to hit him with, or pass to Jason, or even defend myself with, so I just stood there, helpless. Anyway, Jason saw his coat on the bench, picked it up, threw it into the intruder's face, it confused him momentarily and enabled Jason to make a beeline for the knife. There was a terrific fight. They rolled on the ground. Jason managed to take the knife off him, dragged him to his feet but before he could do anything, the man ran off. Jason was going to chase after him, but I urged him not to. I was so relieved to be safe and that he was unhurt, then I gave him a big hug and we quickly left the park.'

Angel said, 'What happened to the knife?'

'Don't remember. He threw it away, I think. I didn't care about that. I was so relieved and so thankful that Jason had been there. You don't know what sort of hooligans are roaming the streets or messing around in public parks these days, do you? Don't you think, Inspector, if Jason hadn't been there he might have killed me? He was so brave.'

Angel nodded then shrugged.

'Did this Richard or Jason say where he lived?'

'No. I don't know, Inspector. I tried to draw him on his address, but he sort of skirted round it.'

'No matter,' Angel said. He had a pretty good idea. 'Was the man with the knife . . . was he wearing a mask?'

Mirabelle Jones stared hard at him, her big blue eyes showing big expanses of white.

'A mask? No. Oh, no. Why would he wear a mask?'

Angel rubbed his chin hard. That was where the stories differed.

'You're sure about that?'

'Positive, Inspector. It would have been much worse if he had worn a mask,' she said, pulling a face of horror. 'I would have been much more frightened! Why would he wear a mask? Oh, no. He wasn't wearing a mask. It was frightening enough . . . oh, no.'

He shrugged.

'No matter.'

'And what did you do then?'

She looked awkwardly at him then smiled.

'Well, we got a taxi and went back to his room at The Feathers. He had a bottle of wine sent up and we watched television and that until . . . well, it must have been very late,' she added dreamily, still smiling.

Angel nodded knowingly.

'Then what?'

The smile left her.

'I went home,' she said abruptly. 'And I never heard from him again. And now he's dead.'

'Were you unable to contact him?'

'I didn't have his address or telephone number, I told you. I asked him. He said he was always on the move, that there wouldn't be any sense to it. But, in fact, he promised to give me a ring, but I never heard another word. You'd think that after a man had probably saved your life that there would be a special bond, a special . . . very special relationship . . . of a permanent kind, but after a week or two, I began to think something fishy was going on. I didn't know what; perhaps he was married. But, you know, when you think you mean so much to somebody, you'd think they'd keep in touch, but not a word, *nothing!* I got so angry and hurt. I shed a few tears, I can tell you. But, well, time is a great healer they say. When I had heard nothing by Christmas, I wrote him off. Then this morning's paper brought it all back to me. Of course, I was devastated when I read about his death and that he had been . . .'

She trailed off, then quickly reached into her handbag, found a tissue and applied it to her nose.

Angel pursed his lips.

'We need somebody to identify the body. The only relative we could find was his father, but he died just nine days before Richard did. At the moment, we've no next of kin.'

'Oh. How awful. Oh dear. What an awful coincidence,' she said with a sniff. She applied the tissue to her nose again.

'Could you identify him for us?'

Her jaw dropped open. She looked across at him with big staring eyes.

'Oh, I don't know, inspector. I really don't know.'

Angel nodded.

'It isn't pleasant, I know, but there's nobody else to do it as yet.'

Angel thrust his way rapidly along the busy corridors of Bromersley General Hospital. Mirabelle Jones tried to keep up, but teetered precariously on her high-heeled shoes which were causing her to walk pigeon-toed. She sighed with relief when they came to a halt at a large blue door with a sign white on black, fixed to it, that simply read: Mortuary. Angel didn't bother trying the handle; it was always locked. He put his finger to a tiny white plastic button on the jamb instead. Very soon a skinny man in green overalls, white Wellington boots and clasping a long handled squeegee opened the door. He was wearing a white mask over his mouth and nose. He glanced at Angel and then peered at Mirabelle Jones who, seeing only his eyes, gasped, momentarily nervous of him and perhaps in anticipation of the ordeal ahead.

The little man pulled the mask down under his chin.

'Morning, Inspector,' he said, and he opened the door wide enough for them to gain access.

'Morning, Jimmy,' Angel said affably with a wave.

The large room was white-tiled throughout, except for two other doorways at the far end, and the huge frosted windows occupying the wall opposite; four operating tables were set along under the windows with powerful lights suspended over them; near the door, just ahead of them, was a bank of twenty-four large grey metal drawers, some of them with bits of paper stuck on them with pink surgical tape.

The complex smell of ammonia, formaldehyde and body waste hit Mirabelle Jones faster than a demand from the Inland Revenue, and she then understood completely why the man had been wearing the mask over his nose.

In addition, her ear drums were assaulted by the constant buzz and occasional rattle of compressors that produced the refrigeration needed to maintain the condition of the silent inhabitants.

'Hello Jimmy. Is Doctor Mac out?'

The diminutive medical assistant closed the door, leaned the squeegee against the jamb and said, 'Called out to look at some old bones in Pontefract, Mr Angel. Now what can I do for you?'

'I want to show Richard Schumaker to this young lady, Jimmy.'

'Richard Schumaker?' The little man screwed up his face into a squint for a moment, then nodded. 'Yes. Right, sir. I know the one.' He turned to the bank of grey drawers, consulted the paper stuck on one of the drawers and said, 'Yes. Here he is. This is the one, sir.'

He pulled at the handle and with the slightest whoosh of steel balls rolling on well oiled bearings, the drawer slid out accompanied by a cloud of cold air that billowed at first then dropped down to form several concentrated streams that drifted down to the floor like channels of water in a waterfall.

Jimmy had pulled the drawer out only about a third of the way and was still holding on to the handle.

Mirabelle took in a deep breath and looked down at the shape of the head and shoulders of a figure covered by a white sheet. Angel moved up close to her. He heard her suck in a lungful of air. She put a hand up to her face.

The little man took hold of a corner of the sheet and looked at Angel for the cue to pull it back.

Angel put his arm on her shoulder.

'All you've got to do is to confirm that this is Richard Schumaker, that's all.'

She nodded and licked her lips.

'Are you all right?' he said quietly.

'Yes.'

Angel nodded, and the medical assistant deftly whipped back the sheet to show the head and neck of the young man.

Mirabelle gasped.

The eyes were closed, the skin was shiny, the chin and mouth in need of a shave and now looking pasty white and slightly blue under the eyes, at the temples and round the nose.

She looked down and put a tissue to her nose.

'Well?' Angel said simply. 'Is that him?'

She sniffed and turned away.

He nodded at the attendant, who quickly replaced the sheet over the corpse and closed the drawer.

Angel turned back to the girl.

She looked up at him with moist eyes.

'No. That's not Jason, Inspector,' she whispered.

Angel's face dropped.

'It *is* Richard Schumaker?' he said confidently. 'Isn't it?'

'It's not the man who took me out and wined me and dined me and I went back to his room where I spent six wonderful hours that beautiful day in July. That's not him, Inspector. That dead man is the man who attacked us. The man with the knife. The man who wanted to kill us. He's the murderer!'

Angel's eyes closed momentarily. The corners of his mouth turned downwards. He rubbed his chin.

'Are you sure?'

'Positive. I would *never* forget his face.'

Angel shook his head. His mind ticked away faster than a taxicab meter in a traffic jam. It didn't make sense. The girl was mad or blind or something! She had identified the dead man as the man who attacked Jason, her boyfriend at the time. He understood that Jason was aka Richard Schumaker. The fingerprints on letters from his father matched his. The dead man *was* Richard Schumaker. What she says cannot be right. It couldn't be. It simply couldn't be. The dead man was incontrovertibly Richard Schumaker.

He sniffed and turned towards the door.

He'd had witnesses in the past who had lied all the time, usually finished up being the guilty party, but Mirabelle Jones wasn't like that. She might be stupid or blind or mistaken or confused. She might be in love, but she wasn't a murderer. How come she would rabbit rubbish like this? Everybody knows that this is Richard Schumaker, apparently everybody. Something funny was going on and he didn't like it. Must get down to The Feathers. They might remember this Jason, whoever he is. It's a sizeable hotel; bound to have records. Got the date, 30 July, she said. He hoped she wasn't confused about that.

He heard her say something.

'What's that?' he muttered.

'Where's Jason then, Inspector? Does that mean he's still alive?' she said weakly.

'What?' he growled. 'Don't know. I don't know anything any more.'

'I am the manager. In what way can I assist you?'

'I'm Inspector Angel of Bromersley police,' he said, flashing his warrant card. 'This is Miss Jones. She is assisting me. I'm making inquiries about a young man, who stayed here the night of Saturday, 30 July last year.'

'Oh yes? Mmmm,' the man said, hesitating. 'I suppose that's all right. I'll just have a look, sir: 30 July last year, did you say?'

He turned to a very large book on the table behind him and began to turn back its huge pages.

Angel stood at the desk tapping his fingers impatiently on the woodwork and wished he was somewhere else. The beach in the Maldives would have been first choice, if it had been July, on a long padded deck-chair with a good book and a glass of Old Peculier, with Mary next to him, in a good mood.

Mirabelle Jones stood next to him, beginning to wish she had not come forward with information about Jason, and even more, regretting buying those shoes in the January sales even though they had had fifty pounds struck off the price ticket!

The hotel manager turned round to face them.

'We didn't have anybody staying that night. It was a Saturday. Very slack night here, sir. Usually ram-jam full from Monday to Friday with businessmen, reps and so on. Every room occupied. Nobody stayed with us that Saturday night.'

Angel turned to Mirabelle Jones.

She looked up at him with doleful eyes.

'He *was* staying here that night, Inspector,' she said firmly out of the side of her mouth, avoiding the hotel manager's eyes. 'I was in the room with him. I should know,' she said impatiently.

Angel rubbed his chin.

'Do you remember the room number?'

'No.'

Angel turned back to the man.

'Were you on duty that day, by any chance?'

He referred back to the big book.

'No. It was a new man, a trainee, a Mr Page.'

'I'd like to see him, then,' Angel said resolutely.

'I'm afraid that's not possible. He proved to be . . . unsuitable. I'm afraid I had to, erm, let him go.'

Angel sniffed.

'Let him go? You mean you gave him the sack?' he growled.

'Well . . . yes.'

Angel wrinkled his nose.

'Hmmm. Well, where is he now?'

'I really couldn't say, sir.'

'*You really couldn't say?*' Angel bellowed.

A couple passing and two men coming out of the lift turned their heads and stared at him.

'I really couldn't say, sir,' the man repeated coolly.

Mirabelle Jones saw Angel's neck turn the colour of her favourite lipstick.

'Do you mean you don't know?' he said, glowering at him.

'Well . . . yes.'

Angel grunted.

'Well, *why the hell don't you say what you mean?*'

He turned towards the door.

'Come along Miss Jones. This is getting us nowhere.'

FOURTEEN

Angel walked Mirabelle Jones back to his car in silence. He briefly thanked her for coming forward with the information about Jason. It wasn't easy for him, as her statement (which she had made seem absolutely believable) that Richard Schumaker had been her assailant in the park, and not the dead man, contradicted all the evidence he had accumulated up to that point. He couldn't tell her how confused, frustrated and in the depths of hopelessness she had left him. Solving a crime, to Angel, wasn't merely a job of work, it was a career, a challenge, it was his reason for being a policeman; there wasn't any other job in the world he would rather do than detect criminals and put them away. It fulfilled all his interest, his hobbies, his ambitions; it was his *raison d'être*.

He took her address and phone number, offered her a lift to her workplace or home, which she declined, and then returned to the station. He parked in the station car park, entered by the back door, past the cells and up the green corridor towards his office. As he opened the door, the phone began to ring. He was eager to answer it. It could be the latest on Mrs Buller-Price's car. Maybe it had at last arrived at its destination. He reached out for it.

'Angel.'

It was the civilian switchboard receptionist again. She sounded rather distant no doubt recalling the brush she had had with him the day previously.

'There's a lady on the line asking for you, her name is Sharon Rossi. Will you speak to her?'

Angel's eyebrows shot up. This should be interesting.

'Of course. Of course. Please put her through.'

There was a click.

'Inspector Angel?' It was the unmistakable throaty, milk chocolate voice of the beautiful Sharon Rossi.

'Speaking. What can I do for you, Sharon?' he said easily as he slumped down into the swivel chair.

She gave a deep, nervous, throaty cough.

'Just want you to know that I'm . . .

surviving,' she said evenly.

Angel nodded.

'I had every expectation that you would,' he said, his mind flitting around wondering what she really wanted.

'I, er . . . I really did love Pete Grady, you know. I didn't betray him. I have no idea how my mother and Uncle Carl found out that we were in Blackpool.'

Angel knew. He had already worked it out, and he wondered whether he should tell her. He decided he would; the information wasn't that valuable and she might offer some useful dirt in return.

'Oh, I've worked that one out, Sharon. It wasn't difficult really. Pete Grady rang up on his mobile from Blackpool to tell my super that even though he had run off with you away from the safe house, he had every intention of being at the trial and giving evidence as had been originally planned.'

'I was in the room in the hotel when he made the call.'

'Well, my super easily traced the call to a signal from the Blackpool area. He then phoned Solly Solomon, your father's barrister, told him and he passed it on to your uncle or your mother or both. On the principle that people on the run only go to places familiar to them, they would have known the hotel, or wherever, where Pete took you, where he had stayed on a previous occasion, waited for him to come out without you. Then they took him on to the beach and shot him.'

He heard her shudder. He waited then continued: 'And I've also worked out how you found Peter Grady's safe house was in Bromersley.'

'Oh? Oh really?'

Angel thought she sounded genuinely surprised.

'Yes. There were only three people knew the address, Sharon. It wasn't me. So it had to be either Pete Grady or my super. Well, Pete was petrified of your family. As much as he loved you, I didn't think he wanted to take such a risk. That left only one person: Superintendent Strawbridge.'

'Then he was the one who left an anonymous message on my answerphone. He even told me the access code to the back door of the flats,' she said huskily. She sighed and then added, 'I can tell you something else about your wonderful Superintendent Strawbridge.'

Angel's ruse had worked. He listened attentively.

'My mother took great delight in telling me. There's a crook called Mace, Stuart

Mace, who runs gambling clubs in London and some of the provinces.'

'I know him.'

'Well, your Superintendent Strawbridge ran up a debt of a thousand pounds with Stuart Mace that he couldn't pay. Apparently he was a regular gambler. Got the fever, if you know what I mean. Mace sold that debt to my grandfather for £8,000, who threatened to make it known to the newspapers if Pete turned up in court, gave evidence and dad went down. That's why your friend, Strawbridge, tracked Pete and me down and told old Solomon to tip off my mother. Strawbridge must have been greatly relieved when Pete didn't turn up in court.'

Angel pursed his lips. That was interesting.

'He's no friend of mine, Sharon. He's simply my boss.'

'There's no wonder my family hate policemen though, is there?'

He had to agree, but he didn't say so.

'Where are your family now, then,' he said riskily. He thought that even if she knew she wouldn't say.

'No idea, Mr Angel. We have so little in common. I'm old enough and wise enough now to make my own way.'

263

'Of course. And what are you going to do?'

'Well, I'll probably go back to modelling, get some money together until I begin to show. I should have at least five months. I'll be all right.'

'Well, all the best, Sharon. Promise me you'll keep in touch.'

'That's very kind, Mr Angel. And all the best to you. Goodbye now.'

He replaced the receiver.

His mind was buzzing. Now that he had confirmation of some of the questionable activities of the superintendent and some of the reasons why, he must now put the charges to him and see what he had to say in his defence — there might be explanations; Angel couldn't think of any — or go straight upstairs to the chief constable and simply report the facts exactly as they had come to light without embellishment. It was an absolute requirement of the service that he reported the facts promptly to a superior.

This was food for thought.

He leaned back in the swivel chair and gazed up at the ceiling. It seemed rather heartless to report the information to the chief constable without giving the man a chance to explain. But everything seemed so logical, and so cut and dried, he couldn't imagine that there was any explanation, other than the obvious, that Strawbridge was as bent as a barley sugar stick.

There was a loud knock at the door.

He dropped the chair forward and yelled out.

'Come in!'

When he saw that it was Ahmed, it reminded him that the lad was going to be eighteen in a couple of days and he remembered that he had a special gift for him. He kept meaning to bring it, but he always forgot. He must remember. Then he noticed something strange about the lad. His eyes stared. His bottom lip jutted forward unusually. Something was definitely wrong.

'What's the matter? Why are you trying to break my door down?'

Whatever it was, Ahmed could hardly get it out.

'Sir! Sir! He's back,' Ahmed said earnestly.

'What you on about?'

'Superintendent Harker's back, sir,' Ahmed said in a hushed voice as if he was speaking of God. He's in Superintendent Strawbridge's office now. Look's like he's back to stay. And he wants to see you urgently.'

Angel frowned, licked his lower lip and didn't reply. This was strange and very unusual. Old turnip head back after just a couple of weeks. Probably just dropped in to say hello.

Angel leapt up, passed Ahmed at the door and rushed down the corridor. He knocked on the superintendent's office door and pushed it open.

There he was.

Angel's jaw dropped.

'Come in,' called the tall, skinny, ugly, mean, miserable monster himself, Detective Superintendent Horace Harker. He was in civvies, looking skinnier than ever, seated where Strawbridge had been sitting only a few days ago.

'Come in, Michael,' he said with a smile like Caligula used to give to the gladiator as he turned both thumbs down. 'I expect you are surprised. No more than I am. Sit down.'

'What sir? Are you back permanently then?' Angel said bluntly.

Harker screwed up the bushy-ginger-brown-white-and-black eyebrows and said, 'Not much of a greeting for an old comrade is it?'

Angel realized that he must have seemed offensive.

'Sorry, sir. You took me by surprise. Never expected to see you again . . . well, not in that chair, anyway.'

Harker's face immediately changed.

'It's an emergency, Michael. An emergency. Strawbridge has gone missing. Disappeared off the face of the earth. The chief had my application to return here on his desk yesterday, anyway. Enid couldn't settle down there among a load of foreigners. They don't even speak proper English, and she wanted to be near her sister in Wombwell so with Strawbridge gone . . .'

Angel's mouth dropped open.

'Well, sir. Where is DS Strawbridge then?'

'That's it. Nobody knows. Not even his wife. *Nobody* knows. She reported it to the chief yesterday p.m. and, well, here I am. I shall stay at The Feathers for the time being. I have been appointed temporary acting superintendent.'

Angel could hardly believe it. He had really thought he'd got rid of the most miserable and cantankerous superintendent he'd ever known, and here he was — back! And it was strange that Strawbridge had disappeared into the night like that. He wondered what he was up to; it seemed to him that that man was in deep manure.

'Now that's enough explanations,' Harker said. 'Let's get on. I've a lot on my plate. I've to see Asquith and Busby yet. What are you busy with? I understand that Rossi got off. Strawbridge wouldn't like that. Manchester's crime figures will rocket again.'

Angel wondered whether to tell him what he knew about the Rossi family, about Grady, about Strawbridge's gambling, that he was monitoring the location of the car planted by the Rossis at Mrs Buller-Price's farm.

While he was thinking about all that, Harker said, 'You're working on a double murder, aren't you? I've been trying to catch up with all your reports. A young lad at a country club, in broad daylight, in front of a witness. Now that should be easy, and the body of a model found concealed in the suspect's house?'

'Yes, sir. But the suspect is dead.'

'What? Three murders?'

'No. A lad called Schumaker murdered the model and then hid her body in his house. But then later, he was murdered in the country club.'

'Who by?' he said irritably.

'I don't know, sir. But I've just had a witness who has seen his body at the mortuary and says that it isn't Schumaker at all, but is the man who assaulted her and her boyfriend, a man called Jason, six months ago. Furthermore, I have the witness to the murder who says that it is exactly the same MO that was used to assault her and kill Schumaker only last week. The whole thing doesn't make sense.'

'Jason who?'

'Don't know. That's the puzzle.'

'Or a mammoth coincidence. Hmmm. Well,' he said, standing up. 'You're paid to make things that *don't* make sense into things that *do* make sense. Get on with it!'

Angel nodded.

'Right,' he said and turned to go. He stopped with his hand on the open door. He knew he should inform the superintendent about the car monitoring operation at the very least.

'There is one thing, sir,' Angel said, tentatively.

Harker sighed.

'Oh do get on with it,' he wailed impatiently. 'Do whatever it is you have to do. And don't bother me unless you have to. I've still to see Asquith and Busby, catch up with their current cases, and everything else, and report back to the chief. You've been here the longest. You know the ropes. Do what you need to do! Don't bother me unless you have to. This is an emergency situation; surely you can work on your own without me holding your hand all the bloody time?'

That was enough for Angel. His eyes flashed with excitement; his jaw set hard. He was out of that office like a shot. Of course he could work on his own; in fact, he preferred it. And he would rather walk round Bromersley all day with a nail in his boot than listen any more to him!

Temporary Acting Superintendent Harker was blissfully unaware that he had just let one of his inspectors off the hook. It meant that Angel didn't immediately have to report all the incriminating evidence he had on Strawbridge, to him or to the chief constable. It gave him the time and the flexibility he needed to solve his cases his own way, which delighted him. He looked at the clock. It was 5.22. And he wasn't on overtime. He returned to his office with a lighter heart, a song on his lips and a spring in his step. He grabbed his overcoat off the hook, held it in his arms as if it was Ginger Rogers, danced round it three times before putting it on. He flicked the rim of his imaginary top hat then sashayed down the corridor twirling an invisible silver-topped black cane.

The credits at the end of another repeat of a repeat of a repeat of *Only Fools and Horses*

270

rolled up the television screen.

He turned to Mary and said, 'What's on now, love?'

She looked up from her book and muttered, 'Don't know.'

Without looking up, she passed him the newspaper. Angel took it from her and looked at his watch. It was eight o'clock.

The phone rang. They both looked at the phone, then at each other. He pressed the mute button on the television remote and picked up the receiver.

'Hello.'

'Is that DI Angel? Traffic here, sir.'

Angel's recognized the voice. It was DS Mallin. His pulse began to race. This could be what he had been waiting for.

'Yes, Norman.'

Mary noticed his face change.

'That car, sir, it has been standing at a site that, on my map, shows it to be at a four-star hotel between the M1 and the A1, at co-ordinates 676 North and 438 West, for an hour and eight minutes, sir. The name of the hotel is The Yorkshireman.'

Angel's jaw stiffened.

'Right. I know it. Keep monitoring it and in the event of any movement from there, advise me.'

'Right, sir.'

He depressed the cradle for a couple of seconds, then waited for the tone and then dialled a number.

Mary took off her reading glasses and peered at him.

'What's happening?' she said.

'Got to go out, love.'

She wasn't pleased. She looked at the clock unnecessarily and shook her head.

'You'll miss that film.'

'Can't be helped.'

There was a click, and a small feminine voice in the earpiece said, 'FSU.'

'Firearms Support Unit? I want to speak to the duty officer, please. DI Angel, Bromersley.'

'Hold on, sir.'

There was a short wait.

Angel looked across at Mary.

'It's just a little job; won't take long.'

In eight words, he'd told her two lies and he knew it.

'And what's this about "firearms"?' she snapped.

He pulled a face but didn't reply.

'Michael Angel,' an enthusiastic voice came through the earpiece. 'You old son of a gun.'

It was DI White.

'Ah. Waldo. I'm glad it's you. That car has

moved and has settled at The Yorkshireman hotel. It's a posh place on the —'

'I know it,' he said eagerly.

'Good. Can we rendezvous on the main Doncaster Road, about half a mile away this side of it ASAP?'

'Yes. Sure. I reckon we can be there in about forty minutes.'

'How many men?'

'Full complement, I think.'

That was the DI, two sergeants and sixteen constables. Angel was pleased.

'Right, Waldo. See you there.'

He replaced the phone.

Mary said, 'What are you calling out the FSU for?'

Angel was already on his feet.

'Nothing to bother about. Got to arrest some people that just might be difficult, that's all.'

He was out in the hall, grabbing his coat off the peg.

'Be careful.'

'I'm always careful.'

It had been snowing and a sprinkling of the white stuff decorated the gutters and the hedge bottoms on the dark, busy Bromersley to Doncaster Road. It was 20.45 hours. Angel was parked in his BMW tapping his fingers on the steering wheel and gazing every few seconds into his rear mirror. He'd been waiting for six minutes when an unmarked Range Rover and two unmarked Armed Response Vehicles pulled up behind him.

When he saw them arrive, he sighed, picked up a package from the nearside seat, got out of his car and dashed up to the near-side window of the Range Rover.

DI Waldo White smiled and wound it down. From the light of the dashboard, Angel could see that both the driver and White were kitted up in bullet-proof gear with helmets and the word POLICE in white stencilled across them.

'Thought you weren't coming,' Angel said.

White laughed.

Angel wasn't laughing.

'Waldo, the car with the tracer on it has apparently settled, and I believe that in the hotel are three armed people, Gina Rossi and her two sons, Rikki and Carl.'

'The Rossi family,' White said, suddenly serious.

'Yes. I think they're on a final bid to escape the country.'

He passed White the packet he had brought from the car. 'There's a dozen photographs of each of the three of them.'

He took them and nodded.

'What are their arms?'

'Handguns, as far as I know. Rikki Rossi only got off by the skin of his teeth, maybe making for Hull, to catch a boat. I suspect that they've spent the last twenty-four hours loading themselves with all their cash and valuables. Now, if they are alerted to our presence, they will certainly draw their guns.'

White rubbed his chin.

'Not easy. We can't rush them, not unless we know that they are all together and away from Joe Public. The more ordered way would require us to isolate them from all other people, residents, guests, staff in the hotel. I don't want to provide them with any easy hostages. If they spot that they are outnumbered, that's the course they would be likely to take. Can we evacuate the building without them becoming aware of it?'

'Don't know. Public place. Bars and bedrooms. It's not always easy to explain the dangers and difficulties to the public quickly in emergency conditions; they're often there to enjoy themselves, relaxed, unaware of any threat and they don't always appreciate the danger and the need for prompt, silent response.'

White nodded.

'First sign of a uniform and they'll be firing off right, left and centre.'

White said, 'You're the only one not in uniform.'

'Yes. All right. I'll go in and try and sus things out.'

'Are you known to them?' he said suspiciously.

'Slightly,' Angel said misleadingly. 'I can pick them out easily.'

He certainly could. *And they could pick him out at the speed of light.*

'See what I can find out.'

They exchanged mobile phone numbers and Angel agreed to go into the hotel on his own and either return in person or phone back. If he did not come back or phone within ten minutes, White was to bring his team and come looking for him.

He drove his car up the drive to The Yorkshireman. It had an imposing brightly lit front with a dozen or more flags of different nations fluttering over the entrance. He glanced round the huge car-park for Mrs Buller-Price's car. He picked it out among a hundred or more others. It was only a few spaces from the entrance. He parked next to it. He noticed that the number plates had been changed. He shook his head and smiled wryly. He pulled out his mobile and dialled a number.

It was soon answered.

'DS Mallin. Traffic,' a voice said.

'Michael Angel, here. Norman, I want you to organize the recovery of that car from The Yorkshireman car-park *now*. And by the way, the number plates have been changed.'

'No surprise there, sir.'

'It'll have to be wrapped and handled very carefully for SOCO and forensic.'

'Yes. I remember, sir.'

He cancelled the call, pocketed the mobile and strolled boldly up the six wide steps to the revolving door set in the modern stone and glass frontage and pushed his way in. Facing the door was a long reception desk; a pretty young woman was coming out of an office behind it. She saw him approaching and smiled.

There was nobody else about, so he walked quickly round the end of it, pulled out his warrant card, raised the sectioned counter, let himself behind into the area, put his fingers to his lips and pushed the card under her nose.

Her eyes flashed and she backed away from him.

'You can't come behind here, sir,' she said loudly.

'Shhh! Look at this, Miss,' he said holding up the warrant card. 'Look at this. I am a police officer. This is an emergency. Can we go in the office?'

She stood there motionless, her eyes staring, unable to take in what was happening.

'No. No,' she protested.

Angel advanced on her and she retreated further into the office and round the corner out of sight of the reception desk.

'Shhh. Look at this warrant card. I am a police inspector. That's a photograph of me, look.'

She glanced at it quickly then pulled away from him.

'You're a policeman?' she stammered.

'Yes. Can I speak to the manager?'

'He's gone home.'

'Are you in charge?'

'I can phone him. He can be back here in twenty minutes.'

Angel shook his head.

'That's no good.'

'What do you want?'

Angel rubbed his chin.

'You have three guests here, I believe. They are robbers and murderers. They are probably armed and are very dangerous.'

She shivered. Her eyes shone like the taxi lights on a 707.

He pulled photographs of them out of his inside pocket.

'They probably didn't use their real names, it's Rossi, Gina, Rikki and Carl Rossi.' He showed the photographs. She looked at them but didn't seem to see them. She was too afraid and confused to take everything in.

'Not to worry,' he said and took hold of her forearm gently. 'What's *your* name?'

She stared at him for a second. She couldn't answer. She seemed to have forgotten it, then she swallowed and said, 'Carol.'

'Look, Carol,' Angel said gently. 'I have sixteen armed men waiting to come in and arrest them. I have to work out the best, safest, quickest way.'

She blinked and shook her head. She seemed to come out of the trance. Angel's avuncular manner must have relaxed her.

'We had a party of four,' she said, looking down at the photographs. 'They arrived here about an hour ago. Just the one night.'

Angel frowned. He hadn't expected a fourth. It could be difficult if it turned out that Sharon had rejoined the bosom of the family.

'A woman and three men,' the receptionist explained. 'Is she a striking, dark-haired woman with a Caribbean tan, very slim, huge mouth, about thirty-five?'

So Sharon wasn't there. Thank goodness.

279

Angel rubbed his hand through his hair: he could see that the description could very well be how the receptionist saw Gina Rossi. But who was the third man?

'Yes. The two sons were thickset, dark-haired, one about six feet, the other about five feet eight. I don't know who the fourth man was . . .'

She suddenly saw the photographs as if for the first time.

'That's them. That's them!' she squealed loudly. 'The other man was taller and older.'

'Shhh!' Angel said and put his finger across his lips.

There was a noise out in the reception hall. It was followed by the ping of a bell. Angel assumed it would be a visitor with a query. He gestured for her to go and attend to it and to act normally.

She went out.

Angel listened. It sounded innocent enough. Something about a *Daily Telegraph* and a call at 6.45 in the morning.

'Right, sir. Thank you. Goodnight,' Carol said and returned promptly.

Angel said, 'Where are they now?'

'They ordered a meal for the four of them to be served in the sitting-room of 104 on the first floor.'

'For what time?'

280

'Eight o'clock, I think. They'll be in the middle of it now.'

There was some more noise at the reception desk, a man coughed and there was the ping of the bell.

Carol looked at Angel, who nodded and she went out to the desk again.

Angel took the opportunity to contact White. He dialled out the number on his mobile. It was answered promptly.

'Are you all right, Michael?'

'Yes. There are *three* men and one woman, Waldo. I don't know who the extra man is. They are apparently in Room 104 together now. It's on the first floor. Use the stairs facing the door. Come quickly. I think this is a good time.'

'Right.'

He closed the phone and dropped it in his pocket.

The query at the desk seemed to be taking a relatively long time. He listened round the door jamb.

A man with a loud voice seemed to be complaining.

'But I want the bottle, some ice and four glasses, *now!*' he heard him say.

Angel thought he recognized the voice.

Carol said, 'Very good, sir. If you order it from Room Service, they will bring it to your room in the usual way.'

'But I want to take it up with me,' the man bawled heatedly.

She reached out for the phone. 'I can order it for you, sir. It's Room 104 isn't it?'

Angel heard her mention Room 104. That was where the Rossis were dining. He put his head round the door jamb. He recognized the owner of the voice and dodged back. It was too late. The man had seen him. It was Detective Superintendent Strawbridge! No wonder Angel recognised his voice.

'What you doing here, Angel?' Strawbridge said, astonished.

Angel walked through the door into the area. 'Might ask you the same question, sir. All forty-three forces are out looking for you. You left us so suddenly.'

Angel saw him glance towards the stairs on his right and then back at him; suddenly, he made a dash towards them.

Angel couldn't do with him tipping off the Rossis. He lifted up the counter and dodged underneath it. Meanwhile Strawbridge was on the tenth step of the big staircase. Angel spurted up the steps, caught him by an ankle and brought him down. Strawbridge rolled back a couple of steps and Angel dived on top of him. He grabbed his arms but the taller man resisted and managed to break free of his grip.

'What do you think you are doing, man,' Strawbridge growled, then he put his hands round Angel's throat and squeezed.

Angel brought up his clenched fists to try to force Strawbridge's powerful hands away from his windpipe, but he didn't have the angle, so with a mighty effort he pulled up his knees and moved the big man off his stomach. Strawbridge rolled down the stairs to the bottom like a roll of linoleum.

Six elderly residents had gathered round at the foot of the stairs and were looking shocked at the scene.

Angel followed him downwards and grabbed him by the lapels of his coat and pulled him to his feet. He was about to throw a punch at him when he saw DI White push through the revolving doors followed by his team of men clad in navy blue and black uniforms, wearing helmets with 'Police' marked on them and brandishing Heckler and Koch carbines.

Strawbridge saw them also and raised his hands in surrender.

White saw the two men and rushed over to Angel.

'Are you all right?' he said anxiously.

'Yes,' Angel replied breathing heavily. 'Arrest this man. Go straight up. Room 104. Straightforward. The three are together finishing off a meal.'

FIFTEEN

'You've arrested him!' he yelled.

The superintendent jumped to his feet, pushed the chair back away from the desk. 'You've actually arrested a serving detective superintendent in the employ of Her Majesty's Constabulary?'

Angel blinked. He hadn't expected Harker to react so strongly.

'And he's been locked up in a cell in his own station all night?' he continued.

'Yes, sir. Well, he was consorting with the Rossis,' Angel said, trying to sound and look confident. 'He owed gambling debts to them. They are well-known robbers and murderers. It is entirely justified.'

'You'd better have plenty of proof for this high-handed action. In all my experience, I've never had reason to arrest or even argue with my superiors. You come along . . . and . . . I don't know. . . .'

His voice trailed away. He shook his head,

sat down, opened his desk drawer, fiddled around, found a pin and began trying to extricate a piece of bacon from between his teeth.

Angel was delighted with the way the previous evening's operation had gone; all three Rossis and Detective Superintendent Strawbridge were safely locked up in the cells.

'In the car,' Angel said quietly, 'there's all the evidence you'll need to charge the Rossis. There are four doors full of the proceeds of the robbery of that bank, and, no doubt other banks: the banknote numbers will match. That will prove they were there. The prosecution won't have much difficulty showing the probability that Rikki Rossi pulled the trigger that murdered the clerk. Ballistics may be able to show that it was the gun he had on him when he was arrested last night. Also the backseat of that car is stashed with over a million quids' worth of Class A, sir. We've got them for dealing big time, for resisting arrest, carrying firearms without a licence and goodness knows what else.'

The superintendent stared up at him.

'They say the car isn't theirs, that it actually belongs to a Mrs Buller-Price!'

'I can prove that they bought it falsely in

her name, sir, but for themselves. Anyway, their fingerprints are all over it, and I can soon produce witnesses who saw Gina Rossi drive it up to The Yorkshireman yesterday.'

Harker's ginger eyebrows shot up. He pursed his tight thin lips, wrinkled his nose and then said, 'Hmmm. You've an answer for every bloody thing.'

Angel stifled a smile.

Harker sniffed.

There was an awkward silence. Eventually the superintendent said, 'Ah, well, have you got the murderer of that Richard Schumaker yet?'

'No, sir.'

'Have you solved the mystery, an obsession of your own making, of those confounded lucky bags?'

'No, sir.'

'Well you'd better buzz off and solve that case, hadn't you, instead of hanging about here? Frankly lad, *you are just annoying me!* I'll try and sort this Strawbridge mess out and see what the chief says.'

Angel was glad to get out away from Harker and back to his own office. He slumped into the swivel chair and tilted it back, put his legs on the desk and gazed up at the ceiling. He put his hands behind his head and let out a big sigh. He was thinking how much sweeter life would have been if he could have had a mature and happy relationship with his immediate superior. He had hoped for that when 'Old Misery' had moved down to the potteries, and Strawbridge had been posted to Bromersley, but, as events had proved, it hadn't worked out that way. Nothing ever seemed to run on an even path for long. He rubbed his chin and yawned. He was delighted that the Rossis would receive a good long spell in prison — all three of them. They had had a good run for their money, but now they had to realize that the golden days were over. Nobody and no family could ride roughshod over the little people of this country forever, without being caught and appropriately punished. He was resigned to the fact that Harker would have to call him in to tidy up some of the details, but all the evidence was there in the car. And he candidly considered it had been a beautiful piece of police work even though 'Old Misery' would never ever say so.

He wasn't quite clear about what the state would want to do with Strawbridge. The chief constable would, of course, immediately discharge him from the force, but whether the DPP would want to charge him with consorting with criminals, deserting his post, entering into a commercial relationship with crooks, or whatever else, it was too early to say. Gambling in itself was not an offence, but, suffice to say, his career in the police force was over and his image of respectability had been permanently damaged. He would have difficulty in getting a responsible job again.

There was a knock at the door.

Angel hastily swung his legs off the desk, allowing the chair to return him to a business-like position.

'Come in.'

It was Gawber. He looked very animated. His eyes were shining and a hand was waving a small piece of paper.

'Come in. What do you want?'

'Heard about last night, sir. You cleaned up!' he said with a big smile.

Angel wrinkled his nose.

'I wish Mr Charm thought so,' he muttered. 'Sit down.'

Gawber stifled a smile.

'Just heard back from Liverpool CID, sir.'

'Oh yes?'

'Got that number, that mobile phone number from old man Schumaker's address book. They are pretty sure that it will be Richard Schumaker's,' he said, waving the scrap of paper.

Angel's face brightened.

'Ah, now we might be getting somewhere.'

Angel copied the number straight into the memory of his own mobile, and then said, 'See if you can find out the phone company and get a list of calls; that could be very enlightening.'

'I've tried, sir. It's a pay as you go firm, sir. They cannot say.'

Angel pulled a face.

'It's never good for us to get too lucky, is it?'

'Are you going to ring the number now, sir?'

'No I'm not,' he said firmly. 'Whoever has possession of the mobile that answers to this number must be the murderer of Richard Schumaker. I shall ring it only when I get the circumstances right. Don't want to give the murderer advance notice. According to Eloise Macdonald, Schumaker had a mobile phone in the restaurant. The waiter, Dingle, says he neither saw it nor found it there, so Schumaker must have taken it with him into the conservatory. There he was murdered; she fainted, and thereafter it disappeared. SOCO couldn't find it in the conservatory or anywhere in the club buildings or grounds, therefore it must have been taken by the murderer. There is no other

explanation.'

'That is assuming that Eloise Macdonald and the waiter chap, Louis Dingle, were both telling the truth.'

Angel nodded.

'Exactly.'

There was a knock at the door.

'Come in.'

It was DS Taylor from SOCO. He was carrying two see-through envelopes with the word EVIDENCE printed in red across them.

'Ah! Don. What have you got?' he said, opening his arms out to take the envelopes from him.

'Said you wanted them urgently, sir, so I brought them over. Two empty Cheapos Lucky Bags and the torn bits of the photograph that we recovered. We have assembled them on a bit of cardboard as well as we can with Blu-Tack. Neither had any prints or DNA. They were too badly soaked in pigswill.' He pulled a distasteful face. 'Or whatever it was.'

Angel pulled out a dirty, patchwork quilt of a photograph, about six inches by three and a half. There were only about three-quarters of it there, but it was unquestionably a full-length photograph of Tania Pulman in a skimpy dress.

'It had been torn into about thirty-two pieces. We recovered twenty-two of them, mostly from the inside bottom of one of the bins, congealed in the goo; some of the pieces were found on the side of a trough in a sty. The pigs must have eaten the missing bits, sir. We couldn't find them anywhere. We searched high and low.'

'Anything on the back of the photo?'

'No, sir.'

'Any dabs? Any DNA?'

'No, sir.'

'Right, Don. Thanks very much.'

DS Taylor nodded and went out.

Angel picked up the two empty Cheapos Lucky Bags. They had been torn open. He put his fingers inside and looked. There was nothing to see.

'Huh!' he growled impatiently and then rubbed his chin.

'What do they mean, sir. What's the significance of them?'

'Yah!' he bawled. 'I wish I knew. They just keep turning up. Always empty. It's getting very annoying. They turn up in the most unexpected places. There was one hidden behind the mirror with Tania Pulman's body. Obviously Richard Schumaker wanted to conceal it, for whatever reason. Now these, being found in the pigsty, also to be concealed, but this time not by Schumaker. He would have been dead. Somebody else. So who else wanted to dispose of them, secretly? And why? Why? *Why?*'

Gawber knew it was a rhetorical question.

Angel sniffed and tossed them aside. Then he reached out for the tatty photograph. It looked like an incomplete jigsaw puzzle. He peered down at it for a few seconds, then suddenly snatched open the desk drawer and pulled out a hand magnifier. He examined the photograph again carefully.

'Mmmm. I thought so.'

Gawber looked at him intently.

'Spotted something sir?'

'Mmmm.'

He passed the photograph and the glass to Gawber.

'Look closely at the bottom right hand corner.'

'That's where there's a piece missing, sir.'

'Aye. But on the piece to the left of the gap is a handwritten capital "A" followed by a lower case "l". To the right of it are three lower case letters "ove". And below I think I can make out the lower case letters "ania". If the missing piece had not been missing, I venture to suggest that the inscription would have read: "All my love, Tania." '

Gawber looked again at the patched up photograph. After a few moments, his mouth dropped open. He slowly lowered the magnifying glass and said, 'Yes sir. She gave this to a boyfriend or a lover, who subsequently became disillusioned or fell out with her or something, and threw it away in the pigswill!'

Angel pursed his lips.

Friday the thirteenth ended quietly.

Angel arrived home, kissed Mary, ate his salmon, peas and mashed potato, and then sat quietly in his chair in front of the television. But he didn't take pleasure in the programmes. He gawped blankly at the screen. Sometimes his eyes would be closed. There would be a comfortable expression on his face, but he wasn't listening to anything at all. The details of the Schumaker case were in the front of his mind, and his subconscious, like a machine, was assembling the facts and trying all the permutations of how they might fit together.

And . . . to no avail.

He went to bed and soon got off to sleep.

Mary always knew when a case was troubling him. In her experience it was best to leave him alone until he had solved it.

His sleep was fitful. He had been awake

twice. He turned over. His mind wrestled with the case for an hour or more until it was too tired to labour further and then he would fall away to the peace of sleep. He had always been affected in this way. That's probably what made him such a successful detective.

And so the weekend passed with absolutely nothing of interest happening in the Angel household. Mary continued her boring domestic chores while Angel continued his somnambulistic existence, moving from room to room and chair to chair and then to bed as Mary's work schedule and the clock dictated.

On Monday morning, the sixteenth, at 7 a.m., the alarm clock bell rang.

Mary nudged him and switched on a bedside light. Angel automatically threw back the blankets, swung to the edge of the bed, yawned, stretched one arm in the air, tried to scratch a place in the middle of his back, discovered it was impossible to reach, resigned himself to failure, grunted and then fished around for his socks. He found them and his slippers, and put them on. He looked round the room. It was another cold, January morning. Thank God for central heating. In this half-awake state, he shuffled around the end of the bed, out on to the landing, switched on the bathroom light then made his way into the room to the wash basin.

When he was lathered up and had started to shave, his mind started to stir, and he began to think about what he had to do that day. And then, suddenly, like magic, everything became crystal clear. He knew the identity of the murderer of Richard Schumaker. It was as plain as the nose on your face. He also knew the secret of the lucky bags. It was obvious. And he could explain the reason why Eloise Macdonald and Mirabelle Jones told such conflicting stories. He knew why the murderer wore a mask. The fog had lifted. The picture was in focus. Oh, explanations, answers, the whole mystery, everything was rolling out in front of him like prizes in *The Generation Game.*

Sixteen

Angel parked his car at the rear of the station, let himself in with his keycard and bustled up the corridor.

A cleaner washing the floor was squeezing her mop in the top of the bucket. He strode round her and smiled. She looked at him strangely as she thought she heard him singing a song from *West Side Story:* 'I feel pretty. Oh so pretty. I feel witty and pretty and gay . . .'

He danced into his office, took off his raincoat and hung it on the hook at the end of the filing cabinet. He dropped into the chair and immediately stood up again. He felt a bulge in his jacket pocket. Oh yes. He remembered what it was. Mary had put it in there so that he wouldn't forget it. He pulled out the package. It was in a little pink bag and had the name 'Ahmed' written across it in block letters. He had asked Mary to get it for him a week or so ago, but each day he had forgotten to pick it up. He smiled with pleasure and satisfaction as he placed it just so at the end of the desk.

Then he pulled open the middle drawer and took out the file he had amassed on the Schumaker case. He had a lot to do before the rest of the team arrived. He wanted everything to be just right.

At 8.35, he heard footsteps on the corridor outside his office. He looked at his watch, picked up the phone and tapped in a number.

'Cadet Ahaz, sir. Good morning, sir.'

'Ah yes, Ahmed. Good morning. Send DS Gawber in here.'

'Right, sir.'

He replaced the phone in the cradle.

Moments later, there was a knock at the door and Gawber put his nose round.

'You wanted me, sir?'

'Yes. Come in. We're going out to make an arrest,' he said grandly.

Gawber's mouth dropped open and his eyebrows shot up.

Twenty minutes later they were at Frillies Country Club.

Angel led the way up to the reception counter and slapped the palm of his hand on the bell.

Martin Tickell came smartly out of the

back office. The smile on his face disappeared when he saw the two policemen.

Angel was all smiles.

'Good morning, Mr Tickell. You remember DS Gawber, don't you?'

'Certainly do. Good morning, gentlemen. Have you any good news for me? Have you found the murderer of that poor man, yet?'

'Oh yes,' Angel said conclusively. 'Can I have a word with your headwaiter, Louis Dingle?'

Tickell's face dropped.

'Oh dear.'

Angel said nothing.

'Of course. He's in the restaurant setting out the tables for lunches.'

'Would you care to accompany us there? Please lead the way.'

Tickell nodded. He left the counter and reappeared through the office door and led them along the corridor and through the double doors to the restaurant.

Louis Dingle was very smart but in his shirt-sleeves, his coat over a chair, as he seemed to be setting a table. He heard the men approach and went towards them.

'Good morning, gentlemen. Can I help you? Have you come to see me?'

Angel smiled.

'Indeed we have.'

Dingle swallowed.

'I have told you all I know about that poor man.'

Angel nodded and turned to Tickell.

'Is Walter Flagg in the kitchen?'

'He should be. He starts at nine.'

'Yes, he's there, Inspector,' Dingle said.

'Let's all go through to the kitchen, then,' Angel said.

Dingle rushed forward and held open the serving door. Angel and Gawber lead the way and Tickell and Dingle followed close behind.

Flagg was at a bench, pouring some flour into a bowl. He looked up, stopped pouring and approached the party wiping his hands on his huge apron.

'What's all this?' he said with an applied smile. 'A deputation?'

Angel said, 'No, Mr Flagg. I've come to make an arrest.'

'Oh yes,' he said, looking serious and still wiping his hands.

'Yes,' Angel said. 'You see I've solved the mystery of the murder of Richard Schumaker.'

'You mean . . . you *think* it's one of us?'

'No,' Angel said quietly. 'I *know* it's one of you.'

Tickell looked affronted.

The men came together in a half circle in the centre of the kitchen.

Angel said, 'It was quite easy really. There were only four people apart from the victim on these premises when the murder occurred. There was the victim's young lady, Eloise Macdonald, and you three. Well, it clearly wasn't her, although she did confuse me with some of the evidence she gave. But she always spoke the truth. She told it how it was, strange though it seemed to be at times. But she certainly didn't have a motive. So it had to be one of you three. As you may know, Schumaker's mobile phone was stolen at the time of the murder and the day following, I asked each of you if you had a mobile, you each said you had and I asked to see them. I wonder if you'd be so good as to produce them again now?'

Tickell nodded and produced his from his jacket pocket as did Flagg.

Diggle said, 'Mine's in my jacket pocket in there. Excuse me.'

He went out of the kitchen through the serving door to the restaurant. He was gone a few seconds and then returned all smiles. He had the phone in his hand.

Angel then said, 'Be so good as to switch them on.'

'Mine's on all the time I'm at work,' Tickell said.

'So's mine,' said Flagg.

'Mine's on now, inspector,' Diggle said.

Angel nodded and winked at Gawber to check that all three phones were indeed switched on.

Gawber ambled slowly round the back of the three men, looked over their shoulders then nodded back at Angel.

Angel took out his own mobile, switched it on, then went to the memory.

'Whoever's phone rings now,' Angel said theatrically, 'is the person who stole Schumaker's phone after he had murdered him.'

He then pressed the send button.

And nothing happened.

No phone rang.

Gawber looked at the three phones and then at Angel and frowned.

Each of three suspects looked at each other with blank faces.

Angel pursed his lips.

'One of you is not using the mobile he showed me a week ago.'

The three men looked bemused.

'This is the same one I showed you then, inspector,' said Tickell.

Angel said, 'Yes, Mr Tickell. It is. You and Mr Diggle each produced your mobiles

302

from the same places. Mr Flagg however, kept his mobile in his jacket pocket hanging in his locker, no doubt to keep it away from liquids and heat and flour and so on.'

Flagg looked up at him. His eyes flashed.

'Perhaps you would permit my sergeant to take a look there, sir?'

'No!' he snapped. 'There's no need. I only have the one phone.'

Angel's pulse began to race.

'I'm afraid, Mr Flagg, I'm going to have to insist.'

Gawber pulled on a pair of plastic gloves and went across to the end locker. He pulled out some clothes and behind them at the back, wrapped in a yellow duster was a mobile phone. He carefully held it up and looked across at Flagg.

The chef stood there, red in the face and said, 'It's not mine. I don't know how it got there. It's been planted there. I've never seen it before in my life.'

'Switch it on, sergeant,' Angel said.

He pressed the button and it began to ring out, *Brrr brrr. Brrr brrr. Brrr brrr.*

'But how did you know, sir?'

'That's where Flagg kept the phone last time. He wouldn't want it covering with flour. He had to buy another phone so that

303

if he was asked about it again, he could produce that one. He kept that one handy in his pocket, handy in case we went round to check his phone out again. It nearly worked too.'

'But why would he want to steal Schumaker's phone?'

'Because there would be calls to and from him showing the closeness of the relationship he had with Schumaker, which would be — which *will* be highly incriminating. He may also have wanted it in case any of the young women's numbers are in the memory.'

'Will there be a lot?'

'Who knows? But the biggest clue was the list of names with ticks after each one and, ominously, Tania Pulman's name crossed out. You see Walter Flagg and Richard Schumaker had a secret pact. It was a competition between them to make love to as many women as they could. In addition, they each agreed to assist the other to accelerate the game by being a stooge and pretending to attack the virtue of the girl of the moment, permitting the other bravely to chase away the assailant. This had the result of making the would-be lover into a hero and thereby thrusting the girl gratefully into his arms. They changed roles as suited the requirement of the situation. It had been well rehearsed and worked a treat for them. I believe that Richard, however, who was much better-looking than Flagg, stole one particular girlfriend from under his nose. The beautiful Tania Pulman. Flagg may have been already dating her when Schumaker seduced her away from him and killed her while making love. When she went missing, he had to tell Flagg, who must have gone crazy, tore up her photograph, disposed of it in the pig bins, (as he did his blood covered clothes: must have expected the pigs to eat everything in sight) and at the next charade decided to get his revenge by killing him off.'

Gawber shook his head.

'Terrible, sir. Terrible. And what had the lucky bags to do with it?'

'That was where they got the skull and crossbones transfers from; they used the props to impress the girls and make the attacker seem more macho and dangerous. It is also where Flagg found a mask.'

'What did he need a mask for, sir?'

'He didn't want Eloise Macdonald to recognize him. I might never have solved the case if Mirabelle Jones hadn't seen the piece in the newspaper, noticed the similarity in the behaviour of the two men, volunteered the info and then recognized the dead Schumaker as her attacker.'

'I suppose Schumaker intended disappearing when he had sold the house.'

'Yes. And not left any of his fingerprints or DNA around for us to use to catch and convict him when the body behind the mirror was found.'

Gawber sighed.

'A remarkable case, sir.'

Angel nodded.

'Highly remarkable. Right. Check off that phone and let me know what you find,' Angel said, pulling the Schumaker file across the desk. 'You should find numbers that will strengthen the case.'

His eyes caught the little pink packet he had carefully placed there that morning, which reminded him. 'Ah, yes. And send young Ahmed in.'

Gawber smiled.

'Won't be *young* Ahmed much longer, sir.'

'Aye,' Angel said with a smile. 'When is the actual day, Ron?'

'Tomorrow, sir. He'll be eighteen tomorrow.'

The door closed.

The phone rang. Angel picked up the receiver.

'Angel.'

'It's that Mrs Buller-Price, sir,' the civilian woman telephonist said.

'Put her through, please.'

'Ah, Inspector,' she began bursting with news. 'I am so pleased I caught you. I am pleased, nay *overjoyed* to tell you that my Bentley has been repaired by dear Mr Lestrange and that it runs like a bird. It has set me back a thousand pounds, which I have had to borrow from the bank, but that can't be helped.'

'I am so glad, Mrs Buller-Price.'

'So I will not be wanting that new car back; as I said, I have done nothing to deserve it, so if you do come across it, please dispose of it and do what you will with the money. Give it to charity.'

'Are you certain of this?'

'Positive. Certain. Definite.'

'Well, I'll do that and thank you, Mrs Buller-Price.'

'No, *thank you,* Inspector. And you haven't been to see me for ages, Inspector.'

'I'll try and call in next time I'm passing. By the way, there's a reward coming your way, you know.'

'Really? What for?'

'Helping us to catch a notorious gang of criminals.'

'Oh, really. But I haven't —'

'And do you know how much it is for?'

'No idea, Inspector.'

'It's exactly a thousand pounds.'

'Oh Inspector, thank you very much.' She giggled and then said, 'Goodbye.'

He replaced the phone and smiled. Another satisfied customer.

There was a knock at the door.

'Come in.'

It was Ahmed. 'You wanted me, sir?'

'Yes, Ahmed,' he said enthusiastically. 'Come in. Sit down.'

'Yes, sir,' Ahmed said, licking his lips.

Angel thought he looked smart, handsome and had the makings of a fine policeman.

'I understand that tomorrow is your birthday. You'll be eighteen.'

Ahmed smiled.

'Yes, sir.'

'Well,' he said grandly. 'I just wondered what you intended to do with your life.'

Ahmed frowned and said, 'What do you mean, sir?'

'I wondered whether you intended applying to be in the force proper —'

Suddenly, unexpectedly, out in the corridor there was a loud scream. Sounded like a woman or a girl. It was a very loud scream. Then another.

They stared at the door.

Ahmed licked his lips. He jumped up.

'Sir!' he said, and looked anxiously at Angel.

The inspector pursed his lips and then slowly shook his head. It would be WPC Leisha Baverstock again. He leaned across the desk and reached out for the little pink packet with the word 'Ahmed', written on it.

'Here, lad. There's something for you. It will prove very useful, help you in your career here at the station, too. Open it before you go out there.'

Ahmed blinked, looked at Angel, took the little packet and began to smile.

'Thank you very much, sir.'

He tore gently at the paper and peered curiously at the wood and wire that he eventually revealed.

Angel said, 'It's a mouse-trap. You put a bit of cheese on there.'

ABOUT THE AUTHOR

Roger Silverwood lives on the outskirts of Barnsley. After National Service he entered the toy trade where he became a sales director. Aged 50 he went into business with his wife as an antique dealer specializing in Victorian jewellery until he retired in 1997. This is the sixth novel in the DI Michael Angel series.

We hope you have enjoyed this Large Print book. Other Thorndike, Wheeler, and Chivers Press Large Print books are available at your library or directly from the publishers.

For information about current and upcoming titles, please call or write, without obligation, to:

Publisher
Thorndike Press
295 Kennedy Memorial Drive
Waterville, ME 04901
Tel. (800) 223-1244

or visit our Web site at:

www.gale.com/thorndike
www.gale.com/wheeler

OR

Chivers Large Print
published by BBC Audiobooks Ltd
St James House, The Square
Lower Bristol Road
Bath BA2 3SB
England
Tel. +44(0) 800 136919
email: bbcaudiobooks@bbc.co.uk
www.bbcaudiobooks.co.uk

All our Large Print titles are designed for easy reading, and all our books are made to last.